EDGE OF INSANITY

B.J. Woster

<u>**Current titles by this author (more to come)**</u>
<u>Crime Thrillers</u>
36 Hours
Killing Faith

<u>Paranormal Crime</u>
Edge of Insanity

<u>Romantic Suspense</u>
Desires of a Deceiver
Fate's Intervention
Only One
Whispers of the Heart

<u>Time-Travel Romance</u>
Love Through Time

<u>Romantic Drama</u>
Dreamer of Destiny
Victim of Love

<u>Nonfiction</u>
Parenting in the 21 Century: A horror story

<u>Juvenile Stories</u> (ages 6-12)
Ehtaria: a land of their own
I Am Proud of Who I Am (15-book series)

For more information: www.barbarawosterauthor.com

DEDICATION

*For my family, without whose love and support
this book would never have been written.*

ONE

September 1924

"Let me go! Please! Let me go!" Maria implored through the thick, mahogany paneling. Her voice was getting hoarse and weak, but she refused to quiet even though pleading the better part of nine hours had done little to change her circumstances. Her situation seemed as dire as her voice was raspy.

She twisted the doorknob for the hundredth time. Locked. Why she continually assumed, hour after hour, that it would be suddenly unlocked, she could only attribute to the glimmer of hope still firing in the far reaches of her brain. Another part of her brain, less hopeful and full of gloom, taunted that this door would remain locked until her captors came for her, or until she died—from her forced isolation. For it to open before then would take a miracle, which seemed to be in short supply.

She pressed an ear to the wood, cooled by the wind blowing through her open window. It was a cold wind for a summer night, and she shivered, tugging her woolen blanket more snugly about her shoulders. She sniffled and laid her head against the cool paneling. "Please, won't someone help me?" The whispered entreaty would tug at the hardest of hearts, had anyone with a heart been listening, but there was no one listening but her captors, whose voices, faint and uncomprehending, registered through the thick mahogany paneling of her door. She wasn't confident they heard her at all because they seemed oblivious to her appeals; or if they did hear they chose to conveniently to ignore her entreaties, confirming in her mind that they were heartless.

Since she heard their muted whispering, she knew someone was there. Hearing them should have raised that glimmer of hope in her heart; reassured her that she was not alone; yet she could have been buried beneath the earth for all the comfort those whispers provided. She shivered and reached for the doorknob again, stopping midway, a sob of frustration escaping as her hand fell to her side. A momentary surge of anger shot through her, and she lifted her hand, banging against the paneling, but could not find the strength of voice to rail at those standing on the other side. Tears trailed down her cheeks and she stopped her attempts to gain attention, her mind reminding her of the futility of her actions.

She sniffed again, and then pressed an ear against the door, straining to hear the hushed discussion and yet afraid of what that exchange would reveal. The whispered tones scared her. She was scared now more than last night when horrible events resulted in her imprisoned state. An inmate in her own bedroom, held under lock and key by her own father. She was scared now more than when she was nine and the bogeyman came to her in the dead of night and stole her innocence. More scared because escape was out of reach and her fate was unknown.

She glanced at the open window. Her bedroom was on the fifth floor, yet freedom beckoned through that portal, and she longed to answer the silent invitation, as if compelled by an unseen force promising an escape that seemed unattainable. She leaned against the door and slid to stand upon shaky legs. She closed her eyes as she felt the blood flow back into legs unused for the past nine hours, bent beneath her as if in continual prayer; then quickly sank to the ground again as the tingling in her extremities shot painfully from her ankle to her hip. Wincing as the pain intensified, then sighing as it slowly began to subside. When she was confident that she could move again, she stood and shuffled closer to the window and breathed in the heady scent of liberation, tears of sorrow escaping from her eyes. Insanely, she envied those tears, for though the journey was short-lived, those droplets were free to leave their confines and slip away.

Her reason and sanity returned when she gazed down at the greenery far below. If she heeded the silent call and leapt, her fate would be undecided no more—she would be dead. Still, she had to decide whether death would be such a terrible end. Somehow, it seemed a better alternative to what awaited her at the hands of her own family.

The voices outside her door rose ever so slightly, drawing her away from the window and back toward the door. She stumbled over a brown and gray bunny—a gift from her father when she was eight. An appeasement for the innocence he stole from her. She picked it up and squeezed it tight, tears of fear and anguish nearly overwhelming her. How could a man, who'd told her he loved her, every single day for eighteen years of living, suddenly turn so brutally against her? Had not he also been just as loving with her mother, lavishing gifts on his childhood sweetheart—turned wife, and mother? Did his professions of love truly mean so little? Then her mind registered something that shot even greater pain through her heart—his love had always been brutal. For her mother, however, that brutality had been taken to the extreme, but it was she who was now suffering as a result.

She dropped the bunny and stumbled the remainder of the way to the door, her legs giving way in despair as she leaned against the paneling, "Please!" She croaked as loudly as able. "Please, don't do this to me!" She forced herself to go quiet and pressed her ear against the door. Perhaps her fear would be lessened if she knew what fate held in store. The voices were so close now, she could just make out words being spoken, and her heart froze.

"If only she'd stayed in her room after the evening meal, then we would not be having this discussion."

She recognized her father's voice, but to whom was he talking—one of his button men[1]? Perhaps the same goon who'd carried away her mother's body. Oh, how she wished she *had* remained in her room, and remained ignorant of what had happened.

In the hallway outside her door, Arthur Bartonelli breathed heavily, relieved that the pleas of his daughter echoing faintly from

---

[1] Button man: '20s slang for hired killer

behind her door had ceased. He could ill afford to heed her implorations, any more than he could have his wife's pleas. Sympathy he reserved for friends and family, not traitors and enemies. He shook his head at his mental suggestion that Maria was a traitor or his enemy. She wasn't, but she was something just as detrimental to his security—a witness.

He kept his voice elevated and his gaze averted, as if being unable to see the door, or hear her voice, would help shut out the mental image of his daughter, crying and begging on the other side. He'd have already taken care of the unpleasantness, had his son not intervened.

Lorenzo Bartonelli glanced from the door to his father and fought against the urge to flinch. His father's gaze, ever cold and hard, seemed even more so now. As a child, that gaze had terrified him, and still made him nervous on occasion, even though he was a man full grown and had never had a hand raised in discipline against him. He realized, early on, that being an only son, and heir to his father's enterprises, was advantageous, so he had no reason to fear his father's temperamental reprisals. Still, his father had never harmed his mother or sister either, that he was aware of—until now.

Lorenzo closed his eyes briefly to the unwanted image—that of his own wife and newborn son. If his father had finally lost his grip on his mental well-being, could he lash out and harm them should he push this particular issue too far? He'd never been on the receiving end of his father's retribution, but that could change swiftly if stood in the way of the reprisal of his sister. As much as he loved Maria, he loved his newborn son more; and he would never forgive himself if anything ever happened to his precious Rebecca and sole heir, Dante, should Arthur ever suspect any of them of being disloyal. Lorenzo sighed heavily in his mind. How was he going to explain Maria's disappearance to Becca? They were such dear friends, even though nearly ten years separated them in age. What was he to do? He couldn't tell Becca the truth without jeopardizing her life, but knew he needed to think of something in order to save Maria and simultaneously protect Becca and Dante.

He felt a guilt weigh heavy in his heart that he was hesitant to save his sister if it meant endangering his own loved ones. Compounding that guilt was the lack of tears over the loss of his mother. Why did the actions of his father against his mother and sister not faze him as thoughts of harm to his own family? Had what they had done really been so heinous as to warrant the drastic measures being meted? Perhaps his mother's act had, but Maria?

Lorenzo looked into his father's eyes again. Even though his gaze was austere, it was easy for him to see that his father was weary and unhappy over the latest turn of events. Did that tired sadness stem from love or just lack of sleep? It was true that the greatly feared head of the Bartonelli family was growing old, and in this, the wee early morning hour, it showed. It had been a long night of unpleasantness. Now, it appeared it would become an even longer day. Arthur had swept away one disastrous disagreeable incident in the night, only to have another rear its ugly head. Only his sister, Maria, was not ugly. She was a beautiful disaster, but a disaster none-the-less in his father's eyes and he feared, that he would deal with Maria harshly as his father tended to deal with all disasters that stood in his way.

"I understand, Father, that it isn't great for Maria to have seen what she did—"

"Has the other been taken care of?"

"Frank and Carlos came over early this morning and took care of things. They suggested it might be better for all involved if they made a return trip for Maria."

Maria gasped when she heard her brother's voice—at least the muffled voice resembled her brother. So great was her astonishment this his words failed to register. All she felt was hope return. Her brother, always her protector, would never allow anyone or anything to harm her.

"Lorenzo? Lorenzo! Please tell daddy to let me out!" Maria screeched. "I'll be good. I promise!"

"It's probably for the best that they do," her father continued speaking, closing his eyes against the return of his daughter's entreaties.

"We can't kill her and well you know it," Lorenzo's voice rose in rivalry with his sister's implorations. He didn't want to hear her cries any more than his father did, for he didn't want to shoulder a heavier guilt should he fail to persuade Father to change his mind. His mother was gone, and he didn't want to lose his sister too, but how to convince Father to forgo killing Maria also, without becoming his enemy, was the tricky part. No one questioned Arthur Bartonelli's decisions and lived to regret it.

"If I can kill her mother, I can easily dispose of her," Arthur glared at his only son, but his anger was more self-directed. He felt the burden of his wife's death weighing him down, and the thought of having to dispose of his daughter also—it was almost more than he could bear. Almost, but he didn't remain in his position by being weak minded and soft hearted.

"Really?" Lorenzo squared his shoulders and prepared to do battle, reason his only weapon. He took a deep breath, praying he would come out the victor and not another victim. "Just exactly how are you going to explain yet another sudden death or disappearance to the police? Huh, Dad? They're already eager to strap you into the electric chair for the crimes you've committed. Problem is, they haven't been able to prove anything—yet—but once they discover Mother is dead, which they will, they will hound you and every member of this family until they can pin it on you. Tax evasion and your other numerous enterprises may not send you to prison for very long, but murder will. That FBI agent will be begging to turn the lock in the cell door and swallow the key. If he finds out that you're responsible for both their deaths, he'll eagerly fry your ass."

"Damn it all to Hell!" The elder man exclaimed, running short, beefy fingers through his graying hair. "Don't you think I know all of that? Why do you think I have to do something about your sister! Because the FBI *will* hound every member of the family and Maria will be the one to break. We have to do something about her! She's the only witness to your mother's murder. If she were more like you…but she's not like you, is she son? She's not loyal to me the way you are. If you'd been here, you'd have helped me eliminate the threat your mother had become. Maria…well, she just screamed and ran. She ran, Lorenzo. She ran. Would have run straight out the front door and straight to the police." He shook his head and closed his eyes, breathing deep. "She should have known she could never run. If only I could believe that she would never do me harm."

"She has her reasons for hating you, you know."

"I don't give a rat's ass what her reasons are! She should be loyal to the family no matter what the family does."

"I don't think it's what you've done to others that bothers her so much as what you did to her. She's your daughter, for God's sake. If you needed a diversion—"

"Oh, still gnawing on that bone, is she? Well, if she can't understand the rough patch I was going through with her Mom during that time and accept my apology, then she's jingle-brained[2]. I am not going to hang onto that mistake for the rest of my life and neither should she. She certainly shouldn't let it interfere with her loyalty. Loyalty is everything, but she's not loyal, and her mother wasn't loyal. I can't have disloyal people around me. So, Mr. Brilliant Mind, if we can't kill her, as you say, what do you think we *should* do with her? Keep her locked away in her room for the rest of her life? Because I can tell you right now, that's going to be the only way to keep her from ratting me out to the Feds."

---

[2] Addled

"If she hadn't seen you do it, then she might have bought the accident story we planned to give the fuzz[3], but you got careless and let your emotion overrule your common sense. If you hadn't, we wouldn't be sitting here at six o'clock in the morning trying to decide what to do about your only daughter. Your only daughter, you get that, Dad. Don't you?"

"Yeah, I get it, and I get that her mother was my only wife, but that wife was threatening to drop a dime on me![4] I had to do something! If I hadn't, then Vinnie would have. He probably would have strangled her right then and there if he was head of this family. Damn, stupid broad! Now I'm facing the same situation with my only daughter. You think this is easy for me to deal with?"

"You could have handled it better!" Lorenzo snapped and then shook his head in disbelief, "Man, I can't believe that mom bought that line from that FBI agent; pegged her for a pushover, for sure."

"It definitely was a sinker, and if Vinnie hadn't shown up when he did, Sally would have ruined the entire family; had the key to my office in her hand when Vinnie walked in."

"I still can't believe she was going to let that FBI guy go through your stuff like that."

"I can't believe she took that man's word as fact without checking with a member of the family first."

"We'd have just lied to her, like we've always done."

"Yeah, but she'd still be alive—ignorant and alive. Instead, she had to believe an outsider; was ready to allow that man into my private sanctum? Damn, stupid broad! And now, Maria—"

"Maybe Maria will see the light, Dad," Lorenzo said in a last-ditch effort to change his dad's mind. He loved his baby sister, but at the same time, he could see what her testimony, if allowed, would do to

---

[3] Police
[4] Inform the police

their entire family. He could not let that happen any more than his Dad could. After all, he had a family of his own to consider and if his dad went down, he went down. Guilt by association had never felt as heavy a burden as it did at this very moment. "Have you even attempted to talk to her? Or did you just chase her to her room and then lock her in as soon as she shut herself up in there? Maybe we should unlock the door and reason with her. Get her assurances that she won't rat you out."

"No, son, she's too much like her mother. Maybe it runs in their Catholic blood, I don't know—pure as the driven snow and incapable of deceit—both of 'em. Damn shame!"

"Maybe you can marry her off to Uncle Salvatore's son, Giovanni, back in Sicily. He's far enough away to make Maria unreachable. He'd make sure too that no one got to her."

"No, I can't send her anywhere that she might run off at the mouth. Yeah, Giovanni would do what he could to keep the cops away from her, but that doesn't mean she wouldn't seek out the cops when he turned his back one day."

"You're assuming a lot, Dad. Maria may just be scared enough at this point that she'll be willing to have her tongue cut out, if it meant being able to get out of that room and resume her life as a member of this family."

At that moment, Arthur's gaze changed. It took on a maniacal gleam that had Lorenzo worried that his dad would indeed consider cutting out his sister's tongue to keep her from talking to anyone—ever again.

"I hope you're not considering mangling your daughter to keep her silent," Lorenzo whispered worriedly.

Arthur's gaze narrowed and he speared Lorenzo with a look that made it clear what he thought about his son's comment, but he merely shook his head in response, then after a moment spoke again, "No, but I have decided that shipping her away though, that's definitely worth considering. After all, if she goes away, then the FBI can't question her."

"That was my point exactly. There isn't FBI in Sicily, and even if they showed up, Uncle Salvatore and Giovanni would ensure she kept her mouth shut. Besides, you're assuming that FBI guy would even want to question Maria."

"Oh, he'd want to," Arthur sighed. "They always go after the broads because they're the weakest, and Maria's the only weak broad left in this family, but if they find out we have family in Sicily, they'll find a way to get to her. That FBI agent will find Maria as sure as a hound on the trail of a rabbit—*if* we ship her off to family. So, if I were to take your advice and not dispose of her, then the only option is to put her where the FBI wouldn't consider looking for her."

"What do you have in mind, Dad?" Lorenzo's brow revealed his concern over his father's tone, which was far from reassuring. As far as he could detect in that tone, 'sending her away' could mean taking her to New York to bury instead of staying in Chicago. He may not want his sister to topple the family business, but he unquestionably did not want to see her dead, like his mother. "What is it you have in mind, Dad?" He asked again, hoping God would hear his silent prayers and spare his baby sister.

"We'll ship her away, just like you suggested, and I've just thought of the perfect place. After all, there's no better place for a nut than a nuthouse."

Lorenzo winced, for he knew that for Maria, being locked away in a sanatorium was a fate worse than death.

TWO

October *1963*

"Creepy old place," the real estate agent muttered. Thelma Watson did not know what she'd done to piss off her broker, but if he ever offered to front a listing again, she was going to make her answer a resounding *no*. Not that he had offered her any more freebies. She should have suspected something was wrong with the place when he offered the listing with no split commission. Hindsight was always twenty-twenty. She would be lucky to rid herself of this property in her lifetime.

The only thing keeping her from turning away from the listing and paying someone to take it out of her hands was the potential commission. Creepy or not, if she found the right buyer, her commission would just about set her up for life. She glanced in her rearview mirror. This current interested client was only the third serious potential buyer in the three years since she'd eagerly accepted the free referral from her boss.

She spied the place through the trees as her Buick struggled to ascend the long, barely winding road, and sighed. The location alone was a killer and not just to her Buick. It was smack dab atop a cliff overlooking the ocean, on three sides. Although an idyllic setting for those who loved this type of vista, it wasn't ideal for potential business owners. Mostly barren of foliage, the heavy winds coming off the ocean could easily knock over any lightweight individual. She'd thought of planting trees, using money from her own pocket, knowing the commission would easily reimburse the cost; was convinced that trees could ward off the winds and make it a more appealing purchase; but not convinced enough to front the cost. Still, even with the lack of trees, it held a sort of macabre charm.

For the earliest owners, it held an idealism for a different reason. The location was perfect as a tuberculosis facility, and for a sanatorium. There didn't seem to be a threat of mental or sick patients escaping from here unless it was off the side of a cliff. The only other avenue of escape was directly toward the guard shack, which was not a likely course to take for someone seeking freedom. No, it wasn't ideal for a business location, and in her line of work location was nearly everything.

The architecture was not much to look at either. It made her think that when the owner decided to expand, his eyesight went instantaneously dim and simultaneously color blind, for none of the later additions matched the earlier structure.

She shot another glance in her rearview mirror at the Mercedes Benz following close on her tail. With uncharacteristic envy, she noticed that her client's car had no difficulty managing the ever-increasing ascent. She only prayed that once he caught sight of the former home of the Monterey Cliffs Sanatorium and prior to that, the Monterey Cliffs Tuberculosis Facility, he would not turn his car around and drive away.

Rounding the final bend in the road, she was tempted to do that very thing. There was just something about the place… "Creepy."

When she parked her car and cut the ignition, another drawback hit home. Not only was the location a nightmare, but so was the history of the place. Unfortunately, the local townsfolk loved the attention garnered by that history. Stories abounded about unsanctioned and untested surgeries conducted, purportedly in an attempt to cure the patients with TB, and as a way to cure the mentally ill. Then there was the talk about the use of shock therapy on the seriously mentally ill.

More recently, however, there was talk of ghosts. According to what she'd learned, the Federal government stepped in and closed the facility in the nineteen forties because of the atrocities that allegedly sent many of those housed here into the afterlife long before they were ready. Why it took them a decade to decide that the doctor in charge of the facility—Dr. Santanini—was ill-suited to run the place was beyond her comprehension. Some speculation circulating was that the Federal government was well aware of what transpired at the Monterey Cliffs Sanatorium, but did nothing about it, until Dr. Santanini became a victim of a deranged patient.

Whatever the reasons for it finally closing, the rumored hauntings were the reason she was having difficulty selling the place. The townsfolk didn't care though since it was the ghostly rumors which they used to draw tourists to their town. However, it didn't make her job easier. Those tales of ghouls and goblins brought the curious, but never serious buyers, which frustrated Thelma no end. Giving tours to self-proclaimed Ghostbusters and the morbidly curious specter seeker was not part of her job description, but to turn anyone away who was genuinely interested in visiting the place would be tantamount to cutting off her hand before entering an archery contest. If she never showed the place, it would never sell.

Of course, the latest man to take the tour, a doctor also, seemed extremely interested and a review of his financials was promising. He had even told her of his plans to convert the old place into a home for the elderly—if it was to his liking. She prayed, as she collected her satchel, that it would be to his liking, and she'd be able to convince him of the benefits of converting this particular location into that geriatric facility he mentioned.

She pasted on her best professional smile, which she rarely had to fake, and approached the man exiting his car. She normally showed a piece of property with just the right amount of enthusiasm needed to drive home a sale, but in this instance, she liked neither the monstrosity which had been erected behind her nor the monster standing before her, so she had to fake both the smile and the enthusiasm. *These two are meant for each other*, she mused. *Creepy and crabby*.

"What was that?" Dr. Fred Markus asked, his gaze scanning the expansive grounds.

"I hadn't realized I'd said anything, Doctor," Thelma replied hastily.

"Hmm. Perhaps it was just the wind." Dr. Markus turned a full one-hundred-eighty degrees before stopping to face Thelma. "It is a bit windy here, don't you think?"

"That would be because of its proximity to the ocean and the lack of trees surrounding the facility."

"I know what the cause is, Mrs. Watson. I meant it to be more of a rhetorical observation."

Then don't phrase it in the form of a question, you moron, she thought. "Very well," She said aloud, holding tightly to her smile. "Perhaps a suggestion to plant trees wouldn't be out of line, however. That would cut back the strong winds while still allowing a mild breeze to provide a sort of cleansing to the atmosphere. In point of fact, when the previous facility housed TB patients, the lack of trees and the location was ideal since it was believed that people with TB needed plenty of fresh air, which the wind provided in abundance.

"As for the placement of the facility atop this cliff—back in the twenties, during the TB epidemic, it was thought that the germs and bacteria associated with the sickness settled in low-lying areas, so to prevent a recurrence of TB, they built the facility on the highest point available at the time.

"Anyway, just a little history to help understand the reason why this area is treeless, so if you consider the lack of trees a drawback, perhaps tree planting could be included with the renovations and the completion could, perhaps, coincide with the opening of the facility. As I mentioned in our telephone conversation yesterday, this place *was* the first I thought of when you said you were looking for an abandoned hospital-sized facility to house the elderly. All it needs are those trees."

"So you said—repeatedly." Dr. Markus's smile was stiff and his tone with his lengthy monologue irritated. "As to its appropriateness,

I will ascertain that for myself, if you ever deem to begin the tour."

"I do apologize, Dr. Markus. Most of my clients like to know a bit about the place before considering a purchase."

"Yes, well, you can walk and talk at the same time, can't you, Mrs. Watson? Your time is not the only that's precious."

Jackass. "I do apologize. If you will follow me?"

"Whom else would I follow?"

Thelma closed her eyes and counted to ten. *Arrogant, self-centered son-of-a-jackal*, she thought, and the tension began to drain slowly from her body. *Ill-mannered, egotistical know-it-all*, she continued, and her smile became more genuine.

"Since time is of the essence for you," she called over her shoulder as she started at a quick pace toward the front door, "perhaps a cursory inspection of a few floors and the grounds would be best. Otherwise, in a place this large, a complete tour could take several hours."

"I'll worry about my time, you just do what you seem to do best, and talk," the doctor shot back as Thelma pulled a large ring of keys from her satchel and located the one marked *front door.*

Ooh, if only I didn't have to keep my thoughts to myself. "As you wish."

"As it should be."

Thelma closed her eyes again as she felt tension threatening to overtake her body once more. *Brash, coarse, boorish, chauvinistic pig*, she thought and felt the tension subside again. "This first floor was home to the infirmary, the solarium—where the patients with TB came daily for their intake of fresh air—the records room."

"Speaking of records, I heard a rumor that when the facility finally closed, a good number of the patient records were unaccounted for; that there were purportedly more patients than files."

Just great! Here we go again! "You don't seem to me the type of man that would listen to hearsay and rumor, Dr. Markus."

"I'm not. Just thought it might make interesting reading should the records turn up during renovations. After all, nothing like a mystery to peak one's curiosity, and the mystery over just how many people were sent here because of illegitimate reasons is just up my alley."

"If those rumors are true, then I'm sure the files would indeed be intriguing. Now, as I was saying," Thelma continued, making her way through the doorway of the expansive kitchen area. "The first floor also housed the kitchen, which as you can see, should be quite sufficient for your needs, should you decide to convert the place into that geriatric facility you mentioned."

"I'm not a cook, so my needs wouldn't be filled here."

"Of course not." Thelma tried to keep the sarcasm out of her tone, but it was becoming increasingly difficult. "Is there a particular room you would be interested in visiting, Dr. Markus?"

"The surgery room. The Autopsy room, perhaps," Dr. Markus replied without hesitation.

"But of course. This way, please. That would be on the second floor."

"How many stories are there in this place again?"

"Six."

"To save time why don't you tell me what each floor was used for?"

I was getting to that. Thelma flipped through the keys on her ring to locate the smallest one for the elevator. She turned the key and winced when the screeching sound of disuse reached her ears.

"Keyed elevator?" The doctor observed.

"This facility was built in the late eighteen hundreds when elevators relied upon elevator operators to ferry passengers between floors. If you intend to keep this elevator, you'll need to hire—"

"I'll replace it," the doctor interrupted. "Relying upon a full-time person to operate an elevator seems impractical."

"Indeed," Thelma agreed, surprised he was more concerned with hiring an operator than the cost of replacing the entire elevator unit. Still, anyone who could afford this place wasn't hard up for cash. They stood and waited for the elevator car to make its way slowly to their floor, so Thelma continued her verbal explanation, "As I mentioned, the second floor housed the surgery, recovery room—if you can call it that—and the autopsy room. Um…you know, it may be faster to take the stairs rather than wait for the elevator."

"Was the shudder passing through you because of a particular reason, Mrs. Watson?"

"Just a chill from a draft somewhere," Thelma lied. In reality it was the thought of climbing into that rickety elevator that had her shivering. She recalled the first time she showed the property and utilized the elevator, her knees had knocked the entire time with fear that the cables would snap on her and the other occupant. The second time she showed the property, she made straight for the staircase, but the person—severely obese—refused, insisting on taking the elevator. Being squeezed in the tiny box with a man topping four hundred pounds had given Thelma nightmares for weeks. Since that time, she'd shaken off the fear of the elevator as much as able, but still made the suggestion that the staircase would be a better option, which no one ever took her up on. Now, as she listened to the creaks and groans of the approaching car, she shivered again.

"Certainly *you* haven't been listening to rumors circulating about the autopsy room, have you?" Dr. Markus teased, mistaking her reason for feeling nervous.

The insensitive clod is actually laughing at my discomfort. Oh, if my desperation to rid myself of this place was not so great, I would use words no lady should and storm right out the front door. That would teach him a thing or two, she thought. *Or not.* He did not seem the sort to be upset over a woman's temper tantrum. He'd probably call her boss and have her fired though. She smiled thinly and entered the elevator ahead of him. "I see you've heard those rumors as well. Well, this is one instance where the rumors are closer to reality—as you will soon see—so when you know the history, seeing the residual effects can make almost anyone shudder."

The doors screeched open and they stepped inside. Thelma resisted the urge to lean against the wall as she pulled the barrier gate closed. She put the key into the panel and pressed the faded numeral *two* and sighed in agitated anguish at the prospect of engaging this man in further conversation. This was her most promising client in three years, but why he had to be a pain-in-the-ass who wanted the grand tour, she could not understand. She must have pissed off someone high up to get stuck with both a notorious property and a noxious client. She sighed aloud and smiled thinly when the doctor glanced at her over his shoulder.

"The autopsy room is actually one of the more interesting rooms in the building—if you like morbid tales, that is," Thelma offered, in an attempt to break the uncomfortable silence. They only had to move one floor, but the age of the elevator prevented a quick ascent.

"By all means, Mrs. Watson, horrify me."

"Well, being a doctor, it probably wouldn't phase you, but a layperson like me might have a hard time coming to grips with the methods used here." Thelma stopped speaking as the elevator screeched to a halt. She pulled the gate open again, and they stepped into the corridor. She continued talking over her shoulder as she made her way toward the room about which they were presently conversing. "Because of the TB epidemic, many of the patients residing here—well, they died."

"And what of the mental patients, Mrs. Watson? Did they live long and happy lives?"

"No, many of them died as well."

"Just checking. Pray, please continue."

Thelma sighed. *Major jackass.* "Anyway," she said, flipping through the key ring to locate the one for the door to the autopsy room. "When patients died, orderlies brought the bodies here, to this room."

"That's probably why they called it an *autopsy* room." The doctor rolled his eyes in a childish fashion. "An autopsy *is* normally how they determine the cause of death."

"Most certainly, but this room was misnomered."

"Ah, you finally caught my attention. How was the room misnamed? After all, there are only so many names you can give a place for determining cause of death."

"Unless cause of death is already established—"

"And something other took place behind this door."

"Precisely."

"And that something other was?"

"Well, as I was saying," Thelma continued, inserting the aged key into the rusty lock, "when patients passed, the bodies were brought here. The surgeons, afraid of the less-than-dearly departed's tainted blood, slit the recently deceased from neck to groin, to drain the blood—that's *after* they jammed the body onto a large hook and hoisted it upside down into the air—to aid in the depletion."

"Naturally."

"Since drainage in an older building is not what it is today and as there were a large number of bodies delivered here regularly—well, the blood tended to pool on the floor before making its way down the pipe and out of the building. So, the tiles, as you will see in a moment," she said, finally turning the key, "are stained a disturbing rust color." She swung the door wide and stepped aside to allow him to pass. "But it was not only human blood that created the hue below your feet."

"Beg pardon?"

"You see. TB was eventually eradicated, so less people were admitted to this place, unless mentally ill. Less people meant fewer deaths, so the owners did what anyone would do—they converted part of the establishment toward other uses, so, the autopsy room thus became a slaughterhouse—for cattle, that is."

"Interesting, indeed."

"Yes, well, if you've seen enough of this room; let's continue on our tour, shall we?" Thelma turned and made her way back into the corridor. She inserted the key to lock the door again. She turned and watched the doctor for a minute, but he just stood staring back. Finally, he broke the silence, but not as Thelma anticipated.

"Why do you that? Seems a bit unnecessary and time-consuming."

Thelma raised a brow and then realized he was referring to her locking the door, "Although I do what I can to prevent vandals coming into the building, it isn't always possible to stop them at every ingress. Therefore, I keep the doors locked. It may not prevent entry altogether, but it does keep someone from entering and destroying every room."

"If they crawl through a broken window—" the doctor started, and Thelma interrupted, following his train of thought.

"Then they can only access the room in which they've crawled into, unless they are so determined that they attempt to kick the doors down. Anyway, as I see it, damage may occur, but only where intruders have access. Without the key, they'd be unable to gain entry into the room, and if they did manage to climb in through a window…well, they'd have to jump back out of that window to get out. They'd have to jump in and out of every window in the facility to do widespread damage, so my locking the door acts as a deterrent of sorts."

"You do like to expound upon details rather extensively, Mrs. Watson. Seems a waste of breath. Still, I'll likely replace the doors also. Carrying around a set of keys isn't my ideal. So, on with the tour?"

When Thelma looked at him in surprise, Dr. Markus arched his own brow in question.

"Um…well…um…indeed. We still have a lot of ground to cover both indoors and out before the day is done."

"You seem surprised that I want to continue explorations. Why is that?" Dr. Markus asked, stalling their departure further.

"Well, to be frank—"

"I would expect nothing less."

"Right…um…well, I've only shown this property to a few serious potential buyers, and…well…I generally don't get past their viewing of the autopsy room before they change their minds and depart. If you are still willing to take the grand tour, you'd be the first person to go beyond the first floor since the facility closed in the early thirties—that I'm aware of, of course."

"Well, that does spark my interest considerably, knowing that I'll be going where few men have gone before," the doctor quipped. "But my curiosity is also peaked over your comment…are you saying you've never investigated the property before, prior to showing it to your first potential buyer? I find that curious indeed."

"I figured I'd be seeing it aplenty during tours, so…since you're still interested, we may want to get to it. Wouldn't want to be here after dark—unless *you* brought a flashlight. The one I brought would barely chase away a shadow, much less illuminate this place at nightfall."

Dr. Markus grinned, "Let's climb back aboard the elevator, shall we?"

Thelma sighed inwardly, but smiled outwardly, and then headed back to the elevator. She started talking too much again, as she always did when her nerves got the better of her, "Now, the third floor housed the TB patients. When they passed, as I've said, they were brought here to the second floor to be tended. The sixth floor was the children's ward, and the fifth floor held the mental patients. Would you care to inspect the patient rooms?"

"Not necessary. What about the fourth floor?"

"Um, well," Thelma stumbled, "we don't really know much about the fourth floor, other than rumor and innuendo. According to the building plans, there do appear to be less rooms on that floor."

"There seems to be a lot of that in relation to this place—rumor and innuendo, that is."

"Yes, well, there isn't really anything there to see, so rumor and innuendo are all there is."

"So, what rumors abound about the fourth floor?"

"Well, there's nothing to substantiate anything—"

"But rumor and innuendo, yes, I know. You've said that several times now. So, again, what rumor and innuendo is bandied about the fourth floor?"

"Well, the rumor is that the fourth floor is…I mean…was—"

"Is this one of those circumstances in which you'd rather avoid telling a potential buyer something which may dissuade purchase?"

Thelma sighed heavily, her cheeks turning crimson.

Dr. Markus sighed also, "As you've probably already discovered, I'm not the squeamish sort, so I'm not likely to turn tail and run if you reveal everything about this place. So…the rumor and innuendo?"

Given the permission needed, Thelma revealed the history in a rush, hoping that if she did so quickly and glossed over it rapidly, Dr. Markus's curiosity would be appeased. "Well, it was rumored that the fourth floor was where the undocumented and unauthorized experimental surgeries and shock therapy took place. It seems that many doctors in the twenties, and a lot earlier, had their own idea of how to cure certain diseases, including diseases of the mind. A sanatorium was a perfect place to find as many of the poor souls they needed to conduct their experiments. After all, many of the mentally ill were the dredges of society, embarrassments that no one would really miss; and as many were kept in a continual state of stupor, they could not very well complain when led to the fourth floor. As for the patients with TB, I'm certain that the doctors truly felt compelled to help them and did what they considered best, but the experiments were experimental, nonetheless, and far from successful."

"It's a good thing you added that last little part or I may have thought you didn't like doctors."

No just you in particular, she thought, but merely smiled thinly in response to his comment.

"So, let's take a peek at the fourth floor, shall we, and then we'll walk the grounds?" The doctor moved toward the elevator. "After all, wouldn't want to be in here after dark. It's still bright out, but very little light filters in through the windows. It'll likely get too dim to tour before much longer."

"Like I said, there's not too much to see."

"I'll be the judge of that, if it's all the same to you."

"Very well, but we'll have to take the stairs."

"What's wrong with the elevator?"

"It doesn't stop at the fourth floor."

THREE

"Now, as you can see, the vista from this vantage is breathtaking. Take a short walk through the gardens and you're overlooking the ocean far below. Of course, since you plan to house the elderly, I do recommend you place a safety railing or fencing along the cliff for their protection."

"Obviously," the doctor replied shortly, and then turned to face the very cliff Thelma spoke of. This was the final area he needed to inspect and then he could make his decision, except— "You'll see about getting a key to the fourth-floor corridor?" He asked conversationally, as he made his way along the wending pathway toward the side of the building.

"Of course, of course, and if I can't procure a key, we can always get a locksmith to replace the lock, or simply have the door replaced, since you think it would be best to do that any way."

"Probably should have already taken care of that point, don't you think? Or did you expect the person buying the place wouldn't want to inspect every nook and cranny before signing on the dotted line?"

"I apologize again. I sincerely thought I had all the keys in my possession." The adage that the client was always right was wearing on her nerves. Still, since she wanted nothing more in her life than to rid herself of this creepy old building, she'd continue to kiss his ass and any other body parts he suggested, if, at the end of the day, she could get him to sign on that dotted line. "I checked the ring myself and I could have sworn the key was—"

"I am curious as to how the builders in the…when was this initial facility built again?"

"Construction of the original building actually dates back to the mid-eighteen hundreds, at a time when sanatoria were being built to house those suffering from tuberculosis. As you know, the owner also decided to open the doors to those individuals considered sick in the head, and so began construction of the upper floors in the latter part of the eighteen hundreds.”

“While I find all that fascinating, I didn’t need a full history lesson. I was simply curious as to why the owner would install an elevator which deliberately missed a floor, or perhaps the elevator operator was simply instructed never to stop at the fourth floor, but…no, that wouldn’t explain why we went straight from the third to the fifth floor, because there’s no elevator operator any longer to prevent an individual from stopping there…it is a curiosity. Well, no matter, I’ll be able to explore that floor as soon as you procure the key, which will permit me to enter from the stairwell.”

“Since you’ll likely want to replace the elevator system with a more modern elevator, the mystery will end with the renovations because the old elevator may not stop at the fourth floor, but a new one—”

“What’s that?” The doctor asked suddenly when he reached the side of the building. He stopped so quickly that Thelma almost collided with him. She sidestepped, moving to stand beside him.

“What’s what?” She asked, evasively.

“It looks like a laundry chute but going into the ocean.”

“Well, can you think of a faster way to get your laundry washed?” Thelma joked nervously. She didn’t want to explain the chute because there was no easy way to explain the chute. And if she did explain the chute, he may decide he didn’t want the place—even if he managed to handle the autopsy room. Still, she shouldn’t be worried over the purpose of the chute since it wasn’t used for the purported purposes today as it was decades earlier.

“Is this like the key?” The doctor asked, watching the indecision race across her features. “Don’t have an explanation for it, so you’ll hope the client will overlook it?”

“No, no, of course not. It’s just there’s the fact and there’s the rumor. I’m required to disclose what I know, but…well…it’s kind of like the autopsy room—more detail than you may care to know."

"I think we've established that I can handle whatever you have to tell me without issue. Okay?"

She did not doubt it. She was almost certain that she'd pegged this man correctly. After all, no one with such a monstrously icy exterior could hold anything less than a frigid heart, so the details of the chute would bother him just as little as the autopsy room did.

"Well, one use was supply and personnel delivery."

"Really? Well, that was a bit of a letdown. I thought you were going to regale me with horror and gore. So, a supply and personnel chute? That seems a bit impractical, seeing as how the kitchen is on the first floor and the origination of the chute is the fourth floor."

"Yes, well, be that as it may, that was its purported secondary use. Um, I guess they found a way to hoist materials up to the fourth floor and then transport them where needed in the facility as any foul weather could close the roads…I don't know. It does sound a bit preposterous, admittedly. It's as though people simply came up with a tall tale to cover up the actual use. Anyway, the supposedly assisted in raising the supplies, which may have otherwise been too hefty for any one man to pull straight up. Also, as there are no other windows along this side of the building, nor any others facing the ocean…well…I'm certain you can see the reasoning."

"Impractical, albeit mildly plausible, but what was the rumored first use, and I assume that you will stress that it is simply a rumor invented by the local townsfolk in order to glamorize the place, correct? Although, the first is likely the actual use, as the second is beyond absurd."

"Yes, well, I would personally prefer to think of the first use as a rumor, since it also borders on the absurd; and as no evidence has surfaced supporting either use as fact, I'll present it as rumor, just as with the second purported usage."

"Safe answer, so what was the rumored usage?"

"Corpse disposal," Thelma replied, and then continued before he could comment. "As you pointed out, the chute originates from the fourth-floor window, where the doctors' experimental surgery was located. Surgery goes bad, dump the body out the window. Someone dies of natural causes; dump the body out of the window."

"What about blood drainage first? Didn't the experimental patients have their blood drained before being hurled out of the window? Isn't that what you told me the autopsy room was for?"

"Not all people here were infected with TB. Those who didn't have TB didn't require draining, so not all bodies were taken to the fourth-floor autopsy room first. Some were simply carried to the fourth floor and—"

"Hurled out of the window."

"That's how the rumor goes, and since some died during treatment within that very room, the body was simply carried over to the chute."

"So that's why you didn't include the mental patients in the explanation of the autopsy room."

"No TB, no fear of re-infestation, no need to drain the body. If a person died of natural causes, which I do believe was rare, the body was carried up and placed in the corridor—"

"Didn't want to interrupt the experiments?"

"I presume something like that."

"So why not just hire a local ambulance service to haul the bodies away?"

It was moments like this when the more-often-occurring ghost seekers questioned her incessantly related to the macabre incidences of the facility, that Thelma was grateful she'd taken the time to learn it's chilling history, "During a certain period of time here at the sanatorium, people were dying—well, left and right, as it were. So many bodies being carried out through the front could very well panic the residents, so to prevent panic they were discarded—well, down the chute. That's what is rumored anyway. Of course, with the currents as strong as they are, no bodies were ever recovered to prove the rumors true."

"Just like the ghosts. No proof, no ghosts."

"No ghosts, so no proof needed," Thelma persisted, attempting to quash another rumor before any more explanations became required. "Still, if it will make you feel better about the purchase, we'd be happy to have someone come in and remove the chute as well."

"No, the chute is fine. After all, I might want to do a quick load of laundry or dispose of a few bodies myself, right? No need to worry about board of inquiries and all that mess." He meant it as a joke. Thelma refused to believe anything but. Still, without the light of laughter in his eyes, it came off as more of a threat. She laughed as a courtesy and turned away. A movement near the back door appeared in her periphery, but before she could bring her gaze to bear, it vanished.

"I suppose all that's left to do is to sign on that dotted line," Dr. Markus was saying. "That is, unless you've suddenly changed your mind about selling the place."

"Not at all, Dr. Markus," Thelma said stiffly, shifting her attention back to her client. "I'll be happy to finally sell it to someone; especially someone with an appreciation of its *twisted* history."

Dr. Markus did smile then, a genuine smile. "Touché, Mrs. Watson. I do believe that you feel you just insulted me. Now that you've derived some sense of vindication for my foul manner, let's return to your office and see about the paperwork, and I trust that you'll have that key for me before the workmen arrive to start renovating?"

"I will certainly make every effort to locate it, yes, but since you're renovating anyway, won't you be replacing the—"

"The doors are solid oak, Mrs. Watson, and, as far as I could tell, still in excellent condition. It would be financially careless to replace something…dear God above!" He whispered suddenly, freezing in mid-step as a ghostly figure ran from the back door. He hugged himself, not merely from fear, but frigidity, as the already cool autumn temperature took a sudden thirty-degree dive.

It was difficult to tell, but from the haunted expression on the otherwise beautiful female's face, he'd have to say that something inside that building terrified her—far more than her sudden appearance terrified him. Though the apparition was several hundred feet away, he could hear her pleas for help washing over him like a winter draft through an open window. He shivered. *You're not supposed to be able to hear ghosts*, he thought inanely, but he did. Her words resounded through his mind— *'help me, save me'*.

His shivering stopped abruptly when a bright red hue near her wrists, stark in contrast to her skin and white robe, caught his attention. She was so far away it was difficult to tell if it was part of her clothing or blood. If it were blood—his clinical detachment reigned in his fear, and he examined the woman emotionlessly. Injury to the wrists would be the likely explanation for bloodied clothing in that area. Attempted suicide, he deduced.

The temperature soared in an instant. The beauteous phantasm was gone.

"Well, so much for the ghosts being rumored," the doctor murmured, unwrapping his arms from about his waist.

"I…I don't know…I've been coming here for three years…I've never seen her, or any other ghosts for that matter," Thelma stammered, still shivering from the sight of the specter running toward them.

"Maybe she wasn't ready to be seen. Or perhaps her attempted flight is done at a time when no one is around to see."

"I guess this mean you'll not be taking the place after all?"

"On the contrary, I'm ready to sign on the dotted line this very evening. All that should be necessary to keep the specters at bay is to have a priest bless the place."

"I don't understand." Thelma's brow knitted in confusion. "You still want to house the elderly here knowing the place is haunted?"

"The elderly doesn't often get visitors once they enter a geriatric facility, so I'm more than certain they'll welcome the company—even if they are of the transparent variety—unless a priest is able to help the ghosts on their way, that is.

FOUR

"Help me, save me!" Maria ran through the back door and into the garden. Her wrists ached and she could feel herself getting more lightheaded as the blood drained slowly from her pierced wrists. She began to wonder at the wisdom of stabbing her flesh in such a suicidal manner, but at the time, she could think of no other way to extricate herself from her room and escape. The infirmary was right next to the back door.

"Help me, save me!" She yelled louder.

He had seen her. The FBI agent had seen her. He turned at the sound of her voice. She ran, swaying, vision blurring. "Help me, save me!" She yelled, but her voice was beginning to fade—too little use, too many drugs.

He was heading her way. She had to let him know that she wasn't insane; let him know what her father had done—to her and her mother; memories that no amount of shock therapy could eradicate.

Although she now lived on the edge of insanity, her brain function was just enough to recognize the agent who indirectly caused her mother's murder. Still, he'd found her, as she feared no one would ever do, and he was her only hope of leaving this place alive.

It had been three years since she'd seen him approach her house to pay a visit to her mother, Sally, that fateful afternoon; a visit that caused her father to fly into an uncontrollable rage and beat her beloved mother to death. Three years since her father sent her away, locked her away in this godforsaken hellhole for witnessing that murderous attack.

Today though was not hellhole day, it was recreation day in the solarium. Not that there was anything entertaining about sitting around in a half-drugged stupor staring out the window, knowing your freedom is only an inattentive guard away. Maria had seen the agent talking to Dr. Santanini earlier. Recognition speared through her chlorpromazine-induced fog, and she felt suddenly alert. She'd moved toward the door of the recreation room but before she could draw attention to her situation, two pairs of hands latched onto her upper arms and dragged her through the side door and into the elevator.

At the fifth floor, they unceremoniously shoved her from the elevator and into room *502*—her personal prison. Then, just for good measure, Jekyll latched onto her arms and held her firmly, while Hyde tore at the hem of her gown. She kicked as much as was able, but it was ineffectual against the two large goons; but as long as there was the possibility that they'd use her for whoopee,[5] she would fight for all she was worth.

The hem of her gown came free with a loud ripping sound, then Hyde bound her hands together. Jekyll shoved her to her knees and Hyde secured the end of the cloth to the leg of the solitary piece of furniture in the room.

"Now stay here!" Jekyll commanded, and then both men exited the room. She was grateful she'd been spared their lascivious attentions, but she was also angry that freedom was just outside, and she was prevented from reaching it.

Desperation spurred the next few moments, for she knew that Dr. Santanini would never permit the FBI agent to visit with her—would deny her very presence—no matter how many badges he flashed in the doctor's face; knew that she had to get to that agent—somehow.

Her father was too well connected; had paid Santanini far too much to allow a federal agent to be within reach of the only person alive that could incriminate him and send him to prison for the rest of his life. She screamed in frustration, pulling at her bindings with all the strength she could muster, but no one heard. She knew no one heard her screams for she'd screamed many times before, and no one

---

[5] To have a good time, especially sexually

ever came to her aid.

In a sudden fit of rage, she shifted her position and rammed her body into the heavy table. To her surprise, the leg broke free. She lay beside the broken leg, stunned at her sudden partial freedom. The same desperation that drove her into the table, spurred another idea as she eyed the sharp shard lying at the heel of one foot.

She snagged the cloth with her teeth and tugged, finally freeing her hands from their ties. With a shudder, she glanced at the shard of wood again, then drew an imaginary cloak of courage about her, allowing determination to overshadow wisdom. If she could only get out of the room, down to the infirmary, then she could make a dash for the door. She had to try.

She heard footsteps running down the corridor. Obviously, Jekyll and Hyde had heard the crashing sound. With no further thought, she jammed the shard as hard as she could muster into her wrist, then yanked it free; the pain threatening to send her into unconsciousness. She screamed in determination and thrust the shard into her other wrist. She tried to shake the pain from her brain, but the shock and agony were too great, and her body started shaking violently instead. Her guards burst into the room and Jekyll winced when his gaze spotted the blood draining from her wrists.

He stomped over and yanked the shard free, uncaring of the continued pain he caused by his actions, shaking his head in angered dismay. He would let her die if it were up to him, his expression disclosed, but it wasn't up to him. With an oath of fury, he bent and scooped her into his arms, then headed down the corridor towards the infirmary.

Maria prayed silently that he would not care enough to do more than follow his normal routine when she or other patients fell ill; and prayed she'd remain lucid so to make it count. She wasn't disappointed. As anticipated and hoped for, the guard dumped her, unceremoniously, on a bench and immediately turned to open the infirmary door.

It was the opening for which she sought. Mustering every ounce of strength, she stumbled for the back door, praying with each faltering step that it would be unlocked. It was. Now, freedom was only a few hundred yards, and a few pleaded shouts, away.

"Please, wait! Help me, please, save me!" She screamed repeatedly, hoarsely, scared that if she ceased her pleas, the agent would turn and leave; but he had seen her and was making his way in her direction. She stumbled and fell. Her damaged wrists scraped and skidded along the cobblestone, and the pain threatened to engulf her in a dark void of insentience, but the sound of the back door banging open against the brick wall helped her to shake the blackness away. She glanced over her shoulder, then toward the agent still moving determinedly toward her. *How far could he possibly be?* She wondered, and pulled herself upright, swaying against the pain and the weakness as a tree in a heavy storm. Though she felt she would topple at any moment, she knew she had to keep moving.

Something in her periphery caught her attention and she let loose a cry of anguish. Besides Jekyll pursuing her, orderlies were heading toward her from the side of the building, and it appeared that someone would intercept her long before the agent got to her. If she could only stay away from the guards, just long enough for the agent to catch up with her.

She pushed herself up onto her feet and stumbled in the only direction free of threat—toward the cliffs.

FIVE

The smell of urine assaulted seven-year-old Mandy Bartonelli's nostrils as she stepped from the elevator into the fifth-floor corridor. She glanced up as her mother's nose wrinkled in disgust as they started down the hall.

"Is it just me, Mother, or does the smell get worse every time we come here?" She was careful to speak softly so as to not offend anyone who may be listening.

"I don't know, Pumpkin," Catherine Bartonelli replied in a whisper. "I can't believe that a doctor as reputable as Jeff Markus would permit the residents of his geriatric facility to live in squalor. I mean, maybe it's just our imagination. After all, the floors look clean, don't they? And this place has only been open for nine years, so it couldn't possibly be in such disrepair as to smell abhorrent, surely. Therefore, we must be imagining the smell; a byproduct of our discomfort surrounding the place."

"If you say so, Mother," Mandy sighed inwardly. That was her mom's reply to any dirty or disgusting place—as long as the floors were clean, then the rest couldn't possibly be too bad; or if we felt uncomfortable, then our imaginations would affect our senses. There was always an excuse. "Do you think it would be possible to take Grannie Becca to the solarium today? At least the windows are always open down there and it doesn't smell as bad."

"I don't see why we shouldn't be able to, Dearest," Catherine replied, stopping in front of her mother-in-law's door. "Here we are. Room *502*," she announced with forced cheerfulness, repressing another urge to shudder, as she always did when she entered her mother-in-law's room. It was not that she disliked Rebecca Bartonelli, or as her family called her—Becca. She liked her a great deal. She had been a good mother to Dante, Catherine's husband—even if she did seem a bit protective of him at times. It was because of that daily devotion, and the family's sense of loyalty, ingrained from birth, that she could understand her husband's wishes that his mother be cared for in her old age.

Grannie Becca had not been devoted and loyal only to her son; she also treated Mandy with a fondness that bordered on obsessive covetousness. Even after Dante passed away, three years prior, Becca continued to dote on little Mandy as if she were her own child and not the offspring of her son. Dr. Markus had stated that it was probably transference; that Rebecca doted so on Mandy because she no longer had her own son in her life. Yet Dr. Markus had not been around, the years before Becca was admitted, to know that the preoccupied doting took place years before Dante's demise. The level of obsessiveness often left Catherine feeling judged and incompetent as a mother, and Catherine didn't like that.

As much as Catherine disliked feeling less a mother in Becca's presence, she genuinely held no dislike for the woman herself. Thus, the shudder of distaste that always gripped her when she visited did not extend from the room's occupant, but from the room itself. No matter what her reassurances to her daughter, she was not at all certain that her mother-in-law was getting the care needed, and she hated that reminder assaulting her nostrils with every visit. It was a reminder that stung because it was she who'd selected this establishment for her mother-in-law to live in.

A thought struck her. Perhaps she could ease her mind by speaking to Dr. Markus personally. Maybe see about moving her husband's mother to a private room with a personal attendant. Of course, she would have to ensure the cost was satisfactory; after all cheap was the main attribute that had initially drawn her to Monterey Cliffs Sanctuary for the Elderly and Infirmed, formerly the Monterey Cliffs Sanatorium. If her husband still lived, Becca would have remained in their family home under the constant care of a private nurse, her every whim catered to. That really sent a shudder running down her spine. She could not see squandering a fortune to care for an elderly relative, loyal and loving or not. To her, it was less cruel to put them away and allow them to live out what little time they had left, full of inexpensive medication, not attempt to prolong their miserable days by hiring expensive care; care that was a waste of time and money, in her opinion.

She was only glad that her husband's will did not specify the kind or cost of care, or she would have had to resort to underhanded means to prevent losing what was rightfully hers. She was still bitter over the proviso in her husband's will that stated she must care for his aged mother. After all, Becca was not her flesh-and-blood. She would not even have bothered with her own mother under the same circumstances—if her mother still lived. Likable or not, she should not have to be responsible for the woman, but her husband ensured that she was stuck with the woman until death. The proviso succinctly and subtly asserted, "Care for my mother or lose my wealth".

If she refused or failed to uphold the arrangement, the family wealth would revert to charity. Catherine shuddered again as she thought of hundreds of millions of dollars, rightfully hers and her daughters, being snatched away to fund an organization to help bring some bird she could not even remember the name of, back from the verge of extinction. Until her mother-in-law kicked the bucket however, she'd worry about it daily.

The first proviso stuck in her craw, but the second proviso really gnawed at her innards. The second proviso required that she maintain open contact between grandmother and granddaughter. Required that, no matter where Grannie Becca resided, she made the effort to visit the elderly woman at least twice a year and every major holiday. She would have been happy sending a monthly stipend, never stepping foot in the place. She grinned wryly—her husband had known her better than she thought.

Dante had been very loyal to his family and wanted Mandy to grow up with the same devotion. Whether she agreed with the loyalty or not, she did understand from where it stemmed. Dante told her, prior to their marriage, about a cruel twist of fate that stole his own grandmother, Sally, away when he was barely out of diapers. He had not detailed that day, only said that his grandmother had died a brutal death and that shortly thereafter, he lost his Aunt Maria as well. Of course, she was not stupid. She knew what had happened. It is what happens anytime one's loyalty comes into question in the Bartonelli family. The disloyal die or disappear. Well, whether she liked the stipulations laid out in the will, she would not disregard them. She liked her life, and she would never put her daughter in harm's way.

"Mother, are we going to go inside the room today?" Mandy watched the emotions play across her mother's face. She knew all too well how much her mother disliked coming to see her Grannie Becca; that she did so only for Mandy's sake, and she knew why. Her mother told her so many times. Told her how it broke her heart that she could not afford better for her mother-in-law or afford a private nurse to tend to Grandmother Becca at their home in Palos Verdes. It cost so much just to raise her only child—food, clothing, and private tutoring were not cheap, her mother said constantly.

She understood and took her mother's hand in her own, "It'll be okay, Mother. What's important is that we are here for Grannie Becca. You can see how happy it makes her when we come to see her, and I'm sure she understands that we can't put her in a nicer place. There is always the option of sending Carmella to help. Maybe she can help to keep her room cleaner, or read to her, or just to provide company more often," Mandy offered.

"We can scarcely afford to let Carmella go, dearest. Who would keep your room clean, hmm?"

"I can."

"I see, and the rest of the house dear? Who would clean the rest of the house? Surely, not you? You have quite a bit on your plate already, Dearest, what with your schooling, piano lessons, dance lessons, voice lessons—"

"Well, maybe not me."

"Well then whom are you volunteering, darling? Surely you don't expect me to do so. What kind of message would that send to our neighbors?"

"I'm sorry, Mother. It was just a suggestion. Perhaps we can go in and see Grannie Becca now?"

"Yes, Pumpkin, I think that's best," Catherine replied, squeezing her daughter's hand slightly.

"Seeing us always makes her happy, doesn't it, Mother?"

"Of course, it does, dear." Catherine turned the doorknob and pushed the door wide, only to be met by an empty bed.

"Excuse me," Catherine called when she caught a glimpse of a nurse outside of her mother-in-law's room. The nurse appeared not to hear and kept walking. Catherine turned to Mandy, "Wait here for me, okay? I'll see what I can find out."

"Okay, Mother," Mandy said softly, her gaze pinned to the bed, made as if never slept in. Catherine stroked her daughter's hair reassuringly, then turned and left the room.

"Excuse me," she called to the nurse who had almost reached the elevator, but the nurse continued ignoring her. "Excuse me," she called louder, "could you tell me where my mother-in-law is?" When the nurse continued to ignore her calls, her temper flared. "How utterly rude." She started down the corridor, now determined to get the woman's name. She would see discipline meted.

When the nurse reached the elevator, she turned, and Catherine stopped dead in her tracks. She felt suddenly cold, only just realizing that the temperature in the corridor had taken a dramatic downward turn. She clasped her arms, uncertain why she suddenly was hesitant to approach the woman standing beside the elevator, who in turn was eyeing her with alarm.

Perhaps it was the thick coil of rope wrapped snugly around the nurse's neck. It looked unbearably tight, but the woman did nothing to loosen its grip. In fact, she wore the noose as a lady of fashion would wear a mink shawl. Her eyes, however, looked haunted. The moment that descriptive thought appeared, Catherine's shivers intensified, wracking her body, rattling her bones. *Certainly, that's not possible,* she thought.

As if commanded, Catherine's gaze strayed downward, widening as she glimpsed the noticeably huge swell beneath the woman's frock. *She's pregnant*, she thought, just as the woman disappeared. The temperature soared high enough to cause tiny beads of perspiration to break out along Catherine's upper lip. Although the temperature climbed, the chill running along Catherine's spine refused to abate.

"Can I help you?"

Catherine screamed, spinning around to face a haggard young woman, standing in front of her, arms full of towels.

The girl took an alarmed step back, dropping the clean linen, "I'm sorry. I didn't mean to frighten you," she apologized, stooping to pick up the towels. When she righted, she noticed that the woman in front of her was deathly pale. "Are you okay? You don't look too good."

"Mommy!" Mandy called, running down the corridor. "Mommy, what's wrong?"

"Didn't you see her?" Catherine asked the maid, her voice barely a whisper.

"See who, ma'am? Are you sure you're okay? Perhaps I should fetch Dr. Markus."

"That's probably a good idea," Catherine agreed breathlessly, and then collapsed near Mandy's feet.

SIX

"Is she going to be all right, Dr. Markus?" Mandy asked the gray-haired physician as she frantically paced in front of her mother, who was lying prone on the black and white checkered floor.

"I'm going to be fine, Dearest," Catherine said in weak reassurance, "as soon as the doctor lets me up off of this rather cold and uncomfortable floor, that is."

"As soon as I've assured myself—and your daughter—that you are all right, Mrs. Bartonelli, I'll do just that," Dr. Markus replied abruptly, kneeling over her, a stethoscope pressed to her chest. "Now, if you all will be quiet for a moment, I'll be able to hear your heart and then I can offer more definitive assurances."

Catherine rolled her eyes in exaggeration and was glad when her daughter giggled. The doctor stood and offered Catherine a hand up, "Well, everything seems to be in working order. Are you prone to fainting spells, Mrs. Bartonelli?"

"Not in the least." Catherine brushed off her navy Chanel skirt. "In fact, this is the first time I've ever collapsed in my life."

"Pregnant?"

Catherine's hand paused in mid-brush. That one word brought about renewed tremors and for a moment she feared she would collapse a second time. The doctor noticed her reaction, the blood drain from her face, and quickly moved to clasp her elbow. "Bring a chair!" He commanded a passing nurse. He turned to one of the other nurses who had gathered because of the spectacle, "Bring a glass of water!"

The nurses scattered like rats before a flood, returning with the items with such haste, Catherine couldn't recall even seeing them leave. She settled into the proffered chair and lowered her head in embarrassment. Nothing had ever affected her in such a manner before, yet here she was fainting at what could very well be her imagination, and overreacting to a single word, just because that imagining happened to *be* pregnant.

"Are you?" The doctor asked, watching her reaction carefully.

Catherine shook her head, "Not likely."

"Mother?" Mandy moved closer to her mother's side, watching her with the same concern as the doctor.

Catherine looked up and smiled reassuringly if a bit shakily. She wiped a hand across her face, tucked her hair behind her ear, and then pulled her daughter into her embrace, hugging her tightly. "I'm all right Darling. I've just never seen a ghost before."

"Ghost!" Everyone exclaimed simultaneously, with the exception of Dr. Markus.

Catherine snorted and shook her head, "A very *pregnant* ghost. A nurse, I believe," she continued with a nervous laugh.

"Perhaps you bumped your head when you fell, making you hallucinate," Mandy offered.

"Sweetheart, it was the hallucination that *made* me faint, remember?".

"Oh, yeah."

"Perhaps it was your imagination just the same," Dr. Markus suggested, but something in his tone brought Catherine's gaze to bear on him, eyeing him suspiciously.

"You know about the pregnant nurse with the rope around her neck, don't you?" Her tone said that he could deny it, but she wouldn't believe him.

"There was a rope about her neck?" The maid gasped, suddenly looking faint as well.

"Bring another chair!" The doctor yelled. "Sandra, do try not to collapse, please?"

"I'll try, sir," she whispered, lowering herself in the second chair, which someone brought as quickly as the first.

"To answer your question, Mrs. Bartonelli—I know nothing about a pregnant ghost. What can you tell me about what you saw? Perhaps it was just a shadow image playing havoc with your sight? Optical illusion?"

"No, she wasn't an illusion. She was so real, in fact, that I thought she worked here. When I tried to get her attention, she seemed to ignore me, so I followed her. When she reached the elevator, she turned, that's when I noticed the rope. It was as if she was planning to hang herself, or did she actually do so?"

"I wouldn't know," Dr. Markus replied, moving to lean against the wall. "I've never seen her."

"But you have seen something, haven't you?" Catherine persisted. There was something about his demeanor that unnerved her—no surprise, no shock, no dismay over discovering his facility could very well be haunted.

"Why it's important for me to admit something of the sort, I don't know, but if it will make you feel better about what you saw, then, yes." Dr. Markus shrugged his shoulders nonchalantly. "Ten years ago, just before I bought the place and a year before I opened it to the elderly, I saw the apparition of a young lady running from the building while I was inspecting the grounds. She appeared injured, but before I could grasp the reality of it, she disappeared."

Catherine was appalled, "Dear Lord above! You knew the place was haunted, yet you still converted it into a home for the elderly? How could you?"

The doctor merely smiled without remorse, "Actually, the agent assured me that it was just my imagination, so I proceeded with the purchase, and since I haven't seen a ghost since that last time—" he let the sentence hang, shrugging his shoulders again.

"But I just have, and what makes you think that your patients haven't seen ghosts? These poor people wouldn't be in any condition to ward off an attack should—"

"If it will put your mind at ease, madam," Dr. Markus interrupted, "I have the place blessed by a priest weekly, so ghosts rarely make an appearance, and if they do so at all, I've yet to hear of it. Did this ghost try to harm you?"

"No, but—"

"And don't you think that if any of the elderly had been harmed in some way, or even haunted, someone would have noticed?"

"Would they?" Catherine whispered softly.

"What was that?" Dr. Markus asked.

"Nothing."

"Listen, Mrs. Bartonelli. If anyone had seen anything, I'm sure that it would have been brought to my attention, and since the last known occurrence was quite some years ago.

"That you know of, and less than ten minutes ago, that I know of."

"Very well, I'll concede that it was years ago, that I'm *aware* of, but still questionable at best, but obviously there doesn't seem to be a huge ghostly infestation. So, we'll just chalk this up to an attention-grabbing experience and move on, shall we? Now, why don't you let me give you something to calm your nerves?"

"No, thank you, I'm fine now. Just eager to leave this particular floor, which we'll do if you'll just tell me where my mother-in-law might be?"

Dr. Markus looked at the nurse, "Sandra?"

"Um, ok." Sandra drew in a shuddering breath, then pulled a small notepad from her pocket. "What room is hers?" She asked, flipping the pad open.

"*502*," Mandy answered.

Sandra flipped the pages of her notebook until she reached the page she was looking for, and then glanced at her watch. "She's scheduled to be in the recreation room at this time."

"Thank you, Sandra," Dr. Markus said, then turned to address Catherine again. "Will you be withdrawing your mother from our facility then?" He asked, seemingly unconcerned about either the specter or the prospect of losing a patient.

"No," Catherine whispered, and for the first time since placing her mother-in-law in the facility, felt a genuine, fleeting, moment of shame.

"Mother?" Mandy whispered, placing a hand on her mother's sleeve.

"Yes, Dear?" Catherine asked, looking down in her daughter's concerned gaze. "It'll be okay, sweetheart," she comforted, before her daughter could speak again. "I don't think that Grannie Becca is in any danger of being harmed. After all, if the ghosts meant harm to anyone, it probably would have occurred before now, don't you think? If they only appear every several years or longer, I don't think there's any need for serious concern, right?"

"Precisely," Dr. Markus concurred, his smugness returning. "Now, why don't you run along to the solarium and pay a visit to your grandmother. I'm certain that she'll be pleased to see you."

"Sounds like the best thing to do," Catherine whispered. Taking her daughter's hand, they headed toward the staircase.

"We're not taking the elevator?" Mandy asked.

"No, Dearest, I feel like taking the stairs," she replied, then glanced over her shoulder. A shudder passed over her when she glanced at the spot where the nurse had stood, directly in front of the shiny aluminum doors of the elevator. She would never forget the haunted expression on her young face, nor forget the rope tightly wound around the petite throat, yet so elegantly draped about her shoulder. She would never forget the swollen abdomen or the child that would never see life beyond the womb. She squeezed her daughter's hand tightly and drew her closer to her side, then opened the door to the stairwell. A final glance back, then she stepped through the doorway and onto the landing, determined to forget—knowing the futility.

SEVEN

September 1927

"How are you today, Maria?" Carol asked, pushing the door closed with her foot.

Maria turned to the voice, a haunted look on her face. "Why do you ask me that? When you know I'm not happy here, that I don't belong here, and that I would give anything for my freedom? Why do you always, every day, ask me that same infernal question, when you know that I'm being drugged and shocked into an unholy submission?"

The smile that had been on Carol's face faded. It was a fake smile in any event, meant to try to reassure those in this wretched place that all was well, when she knew that, in some cases, all was truly unwell—like with Maria Bartonelli. She lowered her head in shame and sadness, wishing, as she did daily, that there was some way to help the few tormented souls not meant to be here. Instead, she ignored the pleas, ignored the endless torture of their lives; reminded herself that without this job, she and her soon-to-arrive newborn would be homeless.

She placed the tray bearing breakfast and medication on the single table in the center of the room, and then turned to look at the young woman, so close in age to herself. Maria should be free, she thought, to live life, love, and have children. Her hand stroked the baby, now moving constantly beneath her frock and the blanket of depression covering her became nearly unbearable, smothering her in its all-consuming totality.

"I wish there was something that I could do for you, Maria," she whispered, but the tone belied the words and Maria sank dejectedly onto the only chair occupying the room. "Please, Maria, don't do this."

Maria's head shot up, "Beg for my freedom?"

51

"It could be worse, you know?" Carol whispered, picking up the vial of chlorpromazine. She prepped the needle then jammed it into the top of the vial, pulling it up until the liquid reached the required dosage. "Please, just take your medicine and then the orderlies will accompany you to the recreation room. The sun will do you good, I'm sure."

"Do you hear yourself? You make it sound as if I'm going on a family picnic. How can you do this? How can you act as if nothing is happening to me?"

The two orderlies, hearing the disturbance, entered quickly, and grasped Maria by the upper arms, restraining her.

"If you truly want to help me, then tell Jekyll and Hyde to let me go!" When she received no response, she stopped struggling and looked toward Carol, who was tapping the bubbles from the syringe. "No! Don't, please?" Maria whimpered. "Please, don't do this. Please, I'll be good. I promise, I'll be good."

Carol rubbed an alcohol swab on Maria's upper arm, desperately trying to block out the young woman's cries. She closed her eyes against a sudden onslaught of pain, stabbing her in the heart. She needed this job; she did *not* need to question whether these patients were being imprisoned here illegally. Without this job, she and her baby would be living on the street, for Dr. Santanini was the only person who had sympathized with her unemployable plight as a young, pregnant—unwed—female; a condition of which, in nineteen twenty-seven would have found her boarding in unpleasant conditions, with no family to rely upon. Instead, she was given room and board at this facility. Certainly, any man who would give a desolate woman a fighting chance would not lock up another female unjustly. Certainly not.

The pain in her heart began to recede, and she opened her eyes, took a deep cleansing breath, and then carefully jabbed the needle into Maria's soft flesh. Depressing the top, she watched with sadness as the hypodermic emptied, as did all emotion from Maria's eyes. She was a helpless shell again, a puppet easily commanded, which the two orderlies did readily, leading her from the room. The engulfing sadness returned. She knew that Maria was the victim of some horrid circumstance, as she herself was, but at least she wasn't locked away and subjected to misery; at least she still had a semblance of a life.

Tears pricked the corner of her eyes as they did every day after her visit with Maria Bartonelli. She was not aware of what had happened to the girl; what she'd seen or done to bring about her forced imprisonment, but she *did* know that the girl did not deserve her fate. The depression that she fought daily, at having to medicate those who didn't deserve a life lived in stupor, welled inside her, but this time she was unable to tamp it down.

"I can't do this anymore," she whispered suddenly, the tears streaming down her cheeks. "I can't continue like this."

Her despair, exacerbated by her expectant state with its whirling hormones, caused her mind to begin shutting down, as if the filament in the flickering bulb within her brain finally burned out. With nothing to guide her but a hand of darkness, Carol strode from the room, looked up and down the empty corridor, and then, as if the blackness determined the next path to take, walked stiffly down the hall and entered the storage closet a short distance from Maria's room. She turned the knob with a strangely steady hand and flipped the switch. As in her brain, the bulb popped, throwing the room into a matching darkness. Carol refused to allow anything to deter her. She stepped aside, so that the light from the corridor could penetrate. After a quick scan of the shelves in the small, cramped closet, she located that for which she was searching, an item she'd seen many times prior and had thought about often. As she hefted the heavy coil, a momentary shaft of light, a hope she no longer cared to nurture, tried to break through the darkness, but she shook it free. No longer did she wish to continue in this life—a life so full of misery and despair for people like Maria.

"I'm sorry, my sweet, darling baby," she whispered, the tears now pouring rivers down her pale cheeks. She continued her one-sided conversation as she made her way back down the hall, "but how can I bring a baby into a world so cruel? How can I live a life of freedom when there are those who suffer so? Please forgive me? I beg of you. Don't hold it against me. We'll still be together; I promise we will." With a cry of anguish and a groan of exertion, she slung the end of the rope over the water pipe running along the ceiling of room *502*. Somehow, it seemed fitting to her to end everything here in Maria's room, but she did not really understand why. All she knew was that it was here that her sadness was greatest, so here was where her sadness would end.

EIGHT

"Grandma Becca!" Mandy called enthusiastically, running across the solarium and straight into her grandmother's embrace. "We didn't know they were bringing you here today, so when we went to your room, and you weren't there—" Mandy couldn't continue. She clung to her grandmother's neck; tears of joy mingled with tears of residual fear.

"Now, now, child," Becca whispered comfortingly, stroking her granddaughter's hair, "as you can see, I'm still alive and kicking, but...Mandy, look at me, dearest." Mandy lifted her head instantly, wiping the tears away with the back of her hand. "Good, girl," Becca commended. "Now, I want you to hear me well, okay?"

"Yes, Grandma," Mandy whispered.

Becca smiled, "You need to understand, dear, that one of these days my life on this earth will come to an end—blessedly, I must admit."

"Don't say that Grandma!" Mandy pleaded, the tears returning. "Please!"

"Now, now, dear, that's enough of the tears for now," Becca reprimanded lightly. "I'm only stating that which is fact, so there is no need to become so distraught. You know, I once heard a man say that we were born to die—but since there is so much time between the two, we should take that time and do something important with it. Not fritter it away. Do you want to know what I've done with my time, child?"

"What Grandma?" Mandy sniffled, wiping at the tears that refused to abate. She loved her grandmother's stories so and hoped that this one would help cheer her up.

"I produced a son, and he gave me you," Becca whispered, stroking Mandy's cheek.

Mandy blushed, giggling "Oh, Grannie Becca. I thought you were going to tell me of a grand adventure."

Becca smiled and sat back in her chair, "It may be a short story, but it is still a grand adventure. Raising children always is, and it made you forget your tears and smile, didn't it?"

"Yes, Grannie," Mandy said with a final indelicate sniff.

"Good. Hello Catherine. Thank you for bringing Mandy," she greeted her daughter-in-law, knowing that the elegantly dressed woman standing before her had no choice but to do her son's bidding. Of course, had she not requested that he add the codicil to his will before he died, she knew without a doubt that Catherine would have vanished from her life the moment of her son's death—taking Amanda with her.

"Hello, Mother Becca." Catherine stooped to place a light kiss on the withered cheek. "How are you feeling today?"

"Spry as a spring chicken," she replied pertly, knowing that her response would irritate her daughter-in-law. Oh! As daughters went, she was a doting one—as long as she knew the doting would end, which is why whenever she visited, Becca did her best to hide her tiredness and age and appear as if everything was right as rain. It took a lot of energy, but it was worth it. She wanted the selfish girl to think that the doting was going to be happening for a good long while yet. Still, while she held a small amount of ill-will toward her son's wife, the obvious love she had for her granddaughter kept those feelings at bay, most times. It was obvious that the love that shone from Catherine's eyes when she looked at Mandy was genuine. What grated on her nerves was that it was evident in Catherine's dress and attitude that she felt herself a station above most in life, and that was not something she wanted Mandy to learn—that stuffy, nose-in-the-air, demeaning attitude. So, whenever Mandy and she paid a visit, she made certain to bring her daughter-in-law down a notch or two, back to where real people lived—at least she tried. Most times Catherine did not rise to the bait. Like today.

"So, what's new with you two ladies?" She said, turning her attention back to Mandy.

"Mother saw a ghost!" Mandy exclaimed.

"A ghost?" Becca exclaimed in proper response, but her eyes were watching Catherine's face as the color slowly drained, for the third time in less than an hour, "Good heavens, Catherine! Sit down, before you fall down, girl!"

"I'm fine, Mother. Mandy, you shouldn't tell people—"

"The truth?" Becca finished, sharply. "Perhaps lying is a better trait to learn."

"That's not what I meant, Mother," Catherine sighed, lowering herself onto a nearby chair. "I just don't feel it's necessary to tell everyone that I've seen a ghost."

"Wouldn't want them to question your mental stability?" Becca grinned.

Catherine just shook in her head in frustration and Becca laughed softly, "So, did this ghost happen to have dark hair and green eyes like you Mandy?"

"Ha! Ha!" Mandy laughed, "I didn't even see her, Grandma, only Mother did."

"Why would you think she would look like Amanda?" Catherine asked. She had heard something in Rebecca's tone when she'd asked about the ghost, something that Amanda missed.

"Oh, I just thought you might have seen your husband's Aunt Maria, my sister-in-law, and your grand aunt, dear child," she finished, glancing at Mandy.

"Oh, wow! Do you think it could have been her, Mother? Do you?" Mandy eyes were alight with typical child-like curiosity. Nothing seemed to disturb her for long.

"I highly doubt that Dearest," Catherine replied, but before she could draw the subject to a close, Becca interjected.

"Oh, but it is highly probable, Catherine. After all, Maria Bartonelli was a patient at this very establishment over forty years ago, only it wasn't a home for the elderly then."

"Really?" Mandy exclaimed, hearing one of her grandmother's famous stories beginning, but Catherine wasn't at all certain that Mandy needed to hear stories about her grand aunt. It was widely accepted in the Bartonelli family that what had happened to Sally and Maria was not to be spoken about; a sentiment that Rebecca Bartonelli did not appear to share.

"Mother—" Catherine started to protest, but Rebecca raised her hand to silence any objection.

"It's time she knows," she said softly. "The family has dispersed. There is no longer the threat there once was about revealing certain truths."

"I don't know, Mother. Some things don't need to be dredged up—especially to a child."

"Sometimes, but I have to disagree about this time. As remaining living matriarch of this family, I feel it's time to reveal that which the Bartonelli's have hidden far too long and who better to know the truth than the future of this very family. Perhaps it will help her become a better, more responsible adult."

"Or it will warp her for the rest of her life," Catherine argued.

Becca arched her eyebrow in disbelief at her daughter-in-law, "I hardly think that will happen. Our little Mandy is a strong girl, aren't you, Dearest?"

"Yes, Grandmother," Mandy responded dutifully.

"And if I tell you something that isn't quite pleasant, will you have nightmares and go mentally berserk?"

Mandy giggled, "Hardly!"

"See, she's not a mental weakling."

"I still don't think this is necessary," Catherine insisted. "After all, the ghost I saw was a very pregnant nurse, and I know for a fact that Aunt Maria wasn't married or pregnant at the time she...well, left the family."

Becca snorted, "That's a convenient turn of phrase. As for the ghost—you may have seen a pregnant nurse, but I personally have had nice long conversations with Maria on numerous occasions."

Catherine rolled her eyes, "Oh, dear Lord above! She has dementia," she whispered. To her mother-in-law she said, in a very condescending tone, similar to one a person uses on the mentally unstable, "Now, now, Becca, all this talk of ghosts has you imagining things. Why don't I call the nurse and have her give you something to help you relax?"

"Oh, do hush, Catherine!" Rebecca snapped. "I'm not dim-witted, girl! Nor am I prone to hallucinations, any more than you."

"Nurse!" Catherine called, standing. She moved toward the hall, leaving a bewildered Mandy sitting next to her grandmother.

"Grandmother, *are* you imagining things?"

"No, darling," Rebecca whispered, leaning forward, "and I meant it when I said that you need to know a few things about your family's tree. Perhaps it will help you to become a better person. Better than your relatives, I hope."

"What was wrong with my family tree?" Mandy asked then scratched her nose. "What's a family tree?"

"That's just a fancy way of listing everyone who's ever been a Bartonelli. Like you." She illustrated by drawing an imaginary tree in the air. "If this were all the people in our tree, from the first Bartonelli until now, you would be here because," she said, pointing to an imaginary branch, way down at the bottom, "*you* are the last of the Bartonelli line. So, in essence, once you marry and take a new name, the Bartonelli family tree will wither and die."

"Wow!"

"So, do you think you're ready to hear about what happened to your great-grandmother and her daughter, Maria?"

"I think so, Grandmother," Mandy said, scooting forward in her seat.

"Okay, but it will have to be the shortened version, because it won't take long for your mother to return with a nurse and end our visit today."

"I'm sorry, Grandmother."

"For what, child?"

"That my mother is so mean to you."

"No need for apologies, Dearest," Becca replied tenderly, "as long as you grow up to be a good person that helps people, and not some stuffy, rich snob, then I'll die a happy woman."

"I will, Grandmother. I promise, I will."

"Okay then, we'll start with why your grand aunt Maria was shipped off to a sanatorium."

NINE

Maria turned the doorknob to her room, constantly aware of the eyes of Jekyll and Hyde on her. She wondered, still in a half-stupor, which one would accompany her into her room today. She hated them for what they did to her, but no one cared. No one stopped them. She also knew that she was not the only one subjected to their unholy attentions. Did her father know what she endured here? Would he care if someone were to tell him? She doubted he even thought of her any longer.

She took her time turning the knob, knowing that the minute she stepped foot into the room, her clothes would be forcibly removed, and she'd find herself pinioned to her mattress, the weight of one of the two men behind her pressing the very breath from her lungs as he released his desires within her hapless body. If only she could stop him, stop them both. If only she could tell someone strong enough to stop them. She sighed inwardly. She was the resident of an insane asylum, which meant that any accusation she hurled would be looked upon as suspicious and chalked up to delusional.

With a last, deep steadying breath, she pushed the door open wide—

And let out a blood-curdling scream.

The two orderlies pushed her aside and moved into the room. Maria fell to the ground, hiding her face in the crook of her arm, her sobs wracking her diminutive frame. She had witnessed only one other thing as hideous—the beating death of her mother; but her mind, doped and weakened, made more of this scene than it normally would have.

"We'll have to go and inform Dr. Santanini," Hyde said.

"Damned shame, if you ask me," Jekyll added, "since she was a good lay, pregnant or not."

"She let you take her?"

"Hell, no! But I had my ways of getting her to take down those lacy drawers of hers."

"Well, I, for one, couldn't bed a pregnant woman, but this one," Hyde reached down and latched a hand onto Maria's upper arm. "This one has more than a nice pair of gams."[6] He yanked her to her feet.

"No!" She screamed, thinking that he planned to take advantage of her in the presence of Carol's hanging body. Poor Carol.

"Not now, keen kitten,"[7] Hyde whispered, pulling her from the room. "I'll wait until they remove that body hanging from inside your room, then I'll have to double dip to make up for lost pleasures."

He pushed Maria down onto the bench beneath the window, "Now you just sit your skirt down right here and don't move. Bobby and I need to take care of a little business and then we'll be right back."

Maria could not have moved even if she'd wanted to, even knowing that they were leaving her alone for the first time since arriving at the facility. She was too distraught, her mind too numb, over walking into her room and seeing the nurse that had brought her food every day for the past three years, hanging there. She readily overlooked the fact that she had brought her medicines too; could not think about that right now, any more than she could about escaping. She pulled her knees to her chest and lie down, a shiver passing over her as her cheek contacted the chilly wooden surface. She closed her eyes against the sight of the body hanging from her ceiling pipes; tried to block out the image of the belly, swollen with child, but the images refused to abate. The tears fell freely down her cheeks and soon she found herself drifting off into a hazy, drug-induced sleep.

---

[6] legs
[7] Appealing woman

TEN

"Hey, dude, do you really think we ought to go up there? I mean, I'm always up for a bit of adventure, but the people in town are really down on the place. Swear it's haunted. Said that so many bad things took place when it was open, that when they finally closed it up, it fell into disrepair faster than a building that size ought to," Joey stated, pausing on the hiking trail just below the 'point of no return' as his friend, Kevin, called it. He pulled out his water bottle and took a swig, stalling as long as possible in the hopes that his nerves would calm before his friends insisted that they move on.

"You ain't gonna go chicken on us, are you, Joey?" Stephen asked.

"Would it really matter if I did?"

"Look, it's likely that it's in tatters now because the doctor that bought it only put enough money into it to make it presentable. That's probably why the feds closed it down and why it fell into the state it's in so quickly," Stephen added, dropping his backpack to retrieve his own water bottle. "Listen, ever since you and I were kids, Joey, we've listened to stories circulate about how horrible this place was—people suffering early deaths due to outrageous experiments, people locked up here against their will—all people talked about was how the ghosts of those dead people roam the halls of that eyesore. That talk draws the tourists to town; keeps businesses—and our folks—from going under. We talked about it all the time at University, so it isn't a surprise about it being haunted. And knowing it was haunted, didn't stop Kevin from saying, 'hey, dude, why don't we rent some ghost-hunting gear and see about making a name for ourselves. Maybe build a theme park in that little town of yours. What do ya say, eh?'"

"Not a bad imitation there, dude," Kevin laughed, "although I'd say I was wasted if I was really talking like that."

"Yeah, well, what I want to know is why Joey here is suddenly so hell-bent on backing out of this when we are almost there? Not to mention leaving would mean losing all the money that we sunk into this gear."

"Look, we were generally three sheets to the wind when we recounted those ghost stories, and nearly the entire time we were planning to make the trip out here—so none of it really stuck in my head, ya know? It all seemed kind of surreal—that we were going to come up here. Since we showed up here, I haven't had much to drink and, well, all the stories that we grew up on are filling up my head with spooks, and I've had little-to-no beer to kick 'em out," Joey whined. "Geez! It still seemed surreal until we actually strapped on the packs and started hiking up. Still don't know why we couldn't break through the barrier and drive up though. That would've been a hell of a lot easier than hauling all this crap up the mountain."

"So, you don't want to go because your head is full of ghosts and your back is killing you. That about sum it up? Cause if that's all there is to it, you're going to have to suck it up and be a man. Kevin and I can't haul all this stuff up there alone, and if we don't go through with this now, we'll lose our money, not to mention never being able to live down being gutless cowards. May as well tattoo 'wuss' on our asses right now. And we couldn't break through the barrier without putting a dent in my very expensive bumper. It isn't as if we could have just picked it up and moved it aside. The owner was serious about not making it easy for people to just drive up here on a whim."

"There may have been a good reason for that," Joey murmured sourly.

"We going to go through with this now, or turn gutless," Stephen snapped, glancing at his watch. "Time's a ticking."

"We go through with this *now*," Joey retorted, "and we may not have any guts left to do nothing with no how, or any part left to tattoo *anything* on. Ever think of that? Didn't all those ghost stories kind of make you wonder if there wasn't something to 'em? Make you think that going into that creepy old place might mean never coming out again?"

"Whoa! Easy dude." Kevin finally dropped his backpack beside the others and plopped onto the damp underbrush, taking advantage of Joey's stalling to rest his legs. "None of the stories you guys ever heard told about involved people getting hacked to pieces. Mainly just sightings and crap like that, right?" Kevin looked at Stephen for confirmation.

"Yeah, that's all we ever heard tell of," Stephen corroborated.

"So, we go up there," Kevin continued, "take a few readings. See if we can't snap some spectral images, hopefully get some kick-ass video, go home, and make a killing on book royalties. Does that sound like a bad thing?"

"Right," Joey sighed, "but if that's all there is to the place how come nobody's done taken those pictures and written that best-seller? How come there ain't already some guy sitting on millions from talk shows and crap?"

"Do you know how many haunted places are purported to be around the United States alone, man?" Stephen asked, and then continued without waiting for a reply. "Millions. So, most people probably stay close to home when going ghost hunting. You and I both know that the people in our town aren't interested in book deals, just feeding the stories to tourists, so they can sell picture mugs and t-shirts. I just happen to want to do more with it than they ever did. Besides, with the roads shut down most times, there ain't too many people willing to hike up to the cliffs to take a tour of the old place. So, seeing as we've already committed ourselves to this, and seeing as how we're more than halfway up the mountainside, *and* seeing as how we need to get to the top before the day gets away from us—why not we just pick up our gear and get it done?"

"Yeah," Kevin nodded, "just think of it this way—the worst that'll happen is that we get so scared, we wet our pants."

Joey chuckled at that thought, "Yeah, right." He bent down and picked up his backpack, then sighed. "Ok. We may as well finish it and get a book deal or two out of it—especially if we're going to be heading back tomorrow with soiled pants."

"That's the spirit!" Kevin laughed, hefting his backpack again. "If it will help any, I bought a six-pack to share when we get there."

"Now you're talking my language!"

ELEVEN

"Dude, this place is really messed up," Kevin proclaimed two hours later, as the three crested the top of the ridge. "Didn't the builder ever go to architect school?"

"Yeah, talk about your archetypal haunted house. It's like the builder knew that it would become haunted one day and wanted to give it an Edgar Allan Poe horror feel," Joey murmured, staring up at the five-story monstrosity.

"Yeah well, I better not start hearing a heart beating from beneath the floorboards or have a pendulum swing down at my head from the rafters," Kevin replied.

"Yeah, looking at this place now," Joey added, "it could easily have been used in that movie of Poe's—"

"House of the Fall of Usher?" Stephen supplied.

"Yeah, that's it!" Joey concurred. "Seriously messed up movie like that deserves a messed-up place like this."

"I've never seen this place up close before. Dang, it's seriously spine chilling! Think it would still be creepy if we didn't know it was haunted?" Stephen grinned.

"Nah," Joey grinned, "then it would just fall into the category of dilapidated."

"Ooh, big words for such a teeny man," Kevin laughed. "Well, I'd say if ghosts wanted a place they could feel at home in, this would definitely be it."

"What's say we get our gear, get our information, and get the heck out of Dodge," Joey said, stooping for his camera, "and has anyone noticed that it just got a hell of a lot colder...ah, crap."

Stephen and Kevin turned to look where Joey's gaze was transfixed. All three watched in morbid fascination as a ghostly image of a man came barreling out the end of a chute protruding from an upper window. They waited to hear the sound of a splash from the ocean below but heard nothing but the hushed moan of the wind.

"That man's already dead," Kevin whispered, tucking cold hands beneath his armpits.

"Duh, of course he's dead," Joey snapped quietly, blowing into his own frigid hands, but Kevin interjected.

"No. He was dead before he went flying out of the window."

Within moments of the sighting, the temperature soared back into the seventies. All three men shivered violently, staring at each other for a moment, as if waiting for someone to declare it all a mass hallucination, which of course they knew it wasn't.

"Now that was some weird crap, man," Kevin whispered. The three men turned to stare up at the chute as if expecting another specter to take a head dive toward the ocean. When it looked like all was quiet again, Stephen turned back to Kevin.

"How did you figure the man for a ghost?" He asked, rubbing the remaining chill from his arms. "And wouldn't that be kind of contrary to a garden-variety haunting?"

"Huh?" Joey crinkled his brow in confusion at Stephen's question.

"If he were already dead, how can his ghost hurl itself out the window? I thought that people only became ghosts when they died violently—"

"What's to say he didn't? And what's to say that *he's* hurling himself out the window? Maybe the men that killed him are in that room hurling him out the window repeatedly."

"So much for non-violent incidents taking place up here," Joey murmured.

"Just because there was violence between them—prior to them becoming ghosts, I mean—doesn't mean they were ever violent to the living, after they became ghosts. If they were, don't you think someone would have said something?" Stephen asked, "And you never answered my question, Kevin. What makes you think that guy was already dead?"

"He wasn't flailing as he was heading toward the water," Kevin answered finally.

"Damn, you're a cool customer. I was too scared to notice anything but the fact that it was an actual ghost."

"Medical student," Kevin said sincerely. "We have to be cool customers."

"We still up to doing this?" Stephen asked.

"We're here now, and at least we know that we have something to see, which means we definitely have something to write about," Kevin said. "Kind of sorry I didn't have the video recorder out already. That would have been some kick ass footage."

"Joey. You still game?" Stephen asked when Joey remained transfixed on the fourth-floor window.

"Yeah, I'm game," he said quietly, "but I'm going to need one of those beer that Kevin brought to fortify my courage first."

Kevin grinned, "Sounds like a plan. Want to drink 'em out here or get inside first?"

"You kidding?" Joey scoffed with a grin. "It's going to take the one just to get me near the front door. I'm going need the second one after we get inside in order to convince my feet to wander around."

"It's a good thing he didn't bring more than one pack, or you'd be so drunk you wouldn't know a ghost if it stood in front of your face and went 'boo'."

"That would've suited me just fine," Joey laughed, "but since that ain't happening, I'll be more than happy to settle for a slight buzz to take the edge off my fear. As long as I can handle a camera, I'll be good to go." He popped the top on the beer and took several large gulps, downing half the contents in one shot. After a quick breath, he tipped the can and finished the bitter brew, then crinkled it up and dropped it at his feet. "All set. Let's get this show on the road."

"You going to leave that there?" Stephen asked, nodding toward the discarded can. "Not very cool to litter, dude," He added in mock seriousness, tipping to finish off his own beer.

"Ah, shut up, priss-pot. Who're you supposed to be, all of a sudden, the litter police?" Kevin jabbed lightly, then deliberately dropped his can beside Joey's. "Gonna call *911* and have them write us a ticket?"

"Go to Hell, Kevin," Stephen retorted, stuffing his empty can in his backpack. "I just don't think you two need to be such damnable slobs." He turned his back on them and headed toward the house.

Joey and Kevin laughed, hefted their gear, and trotted after Stephen. They were half-way across the yard when Joey let out a loud yelp, "Son of a bitch!" A second later, Kevin added his own outraged squeal.

"What in Hell's wrong with you two?" Stephen asked, and then glanced down at the ground. "Ah, crap, this is just too creepy. Didn't you two drop those back there?"

"Hell, yes!" Joey snapped, rubbing at the area impacted by the beer can.

"Then how did it wind up smacking you two in your heads?" Stephen questioned harshly, fear creeping back through the haze already created by his first beer.

"If we knew that, we'd be friggin' geniuses, wouldn't we, Sherlock?" Joey snapped.

"Alright," Stephen replied, drawing in a deep calming breath, "let's just try to chill out, ok? If we can't get a grip, we aren't going to be able to make this trip count for something."

"Yeah, well, you have a poltergeist hurl a beer can at your head and see how calm you stay!" Joey snapped churlishly.

"Wanna go?" Kevin asked softly, still rubbing his own head.

"Home? Hell, yes," Joey exclaimed.

"Look man," Kevin said, "I was smacked pretty good too, and my knees are knocking super loud over the fact that this place really is haunted; that it isn't just a fairy tale told over sales counters to get somebody to buy a t-shirt. Shit man, I think I may have already taken a dump in my pants—twice, so I get it. This is getting way too real, but Stephen's right, we back out now and we lose our shirts—as much as I hate to admit he's right."

Before Joey had an opportunity to respond again, Stephen interrupted, drawing their attention to the side of the building, "Look over there!"

Each tucked his hands beneath his armpits as the temperature took another nosedive.

"Damn, she's beautiful," Kevin murmured.

"Help me! Save me!"

"That's a ghost, right?" Joey murmured softly.

"Yeah, and it looks like she's bleeding," Kevin said, equally soft, his gaze drawn to the red hue on the sleeves of her white robe.

"Leave it to a doctor to notice that!" Stephen whispered. "Hey, our cameras!"

Each snapped out of his trance and reached for the cameras, only to realize the moment had passed when the temperature rocketed to normal. "Crap," the three said in unison.

"We keep missing chances like these and we're going to go home with nothing," Kevin groaned, and headed on towards the front door.

"Maybe that's why no one ever got pictures or made a fortune from this place—always too shocked to remember to do more than gawk," Stephen muttered, as he and Joey jogged to catch up to Kevin.

"Well, I've got my gear out now," Joey asserted, holding up his video camera, and I intend to be ready next time." They each continued to scan the surrounding area expectedly; each ready to memorialize their next ghostly encounter.

"You know, this isn't what I expected at all," Kevin murmured as they reached the front door. "It's nothing like the stories of ghosts that go bump in the night that always circulated around town during tourist season."

"Damn straight," Stephen concurred. "I mean, so far we've had a dead body go hurtling down a chute into the ocean, an angry groundskeeper teach you two a lesson, and a beautiful woman bleeding to death from apparent self-inflicted wounds to the wrists. Just what in Hell happened in this place, and why hasn't the truth of it ever come out?"

"Maybe the ghosts want to be left in peace," Joey offered tentatively. "I mean, if I was a ghost, I wouldn't want someone coming into my domain and stirring things up; maybe trying to make us go toward the light or some such crap." The hue in Joey's pale cheeks deepened at the gazes aimed in his direction. "Well," he snapped, "at least it's viable, and I don't hear any brilliant notions from either of you two dorks! If people were meant to be here in their habitat, why did I get assaulted by a beer can?"

"We already know why—littering," Kevin quipped, but Joey chose to ignore him, this time.

"My mom and dad always said that the ghosts here never hurt anyone," Stephen offered, while he worked to pick one of three locks protecting the front door from being breached, "but that doesn't mean that someone didn't hurt them. Like we said, it's unlikely that ghost hurled *himself* out the window."

"That woman looked like she hurt *herself* though," Joey chimed in, "and if they never hurt no one, why did we get a beer can to the head? And don't say it was because we littered, doofus! Are you sure you can open those?" He concluded, turning his attention to Stephen, who appeared to be struggling with the locks.

"Here, let me try that. I've been practicing picking open locks since we decided to do this thing. I'm confident I can get us in." Kevin stepped over and took the lock picks from Stephen, then answered Joey's query. "Could be someone drove her to suicide and the beer can didn't hurt *that* bad. They may have been playing, or just trying to get our attention."

"Seriously though, if I were a ghost because someone hurt me, or made me hurt myself, I would be out to extract all sorts of revenge on whoever stepped foot in this place," Joey began eyeing the establishment with renewed dread, "so don't expect me to be rooting for you to accomplish your picking those open."

"Then why didn't they ever hurt the elderly people that lived here all those years, when it was an old folk's home?" Stephen asked. "And stop whimpering like a little girl, will ya, Joey?"

"Because they were *old*!" Kevin declared; his lock picking temporarily halted. "Think about it! Many of the people that were here way back in the twenties or thirties, were here because they were infirmed in some way, with TB or mental illness, and then," he continued, leaning back over the lock pick, "some doctor buys it in the sixties and converts it into a place where other old and infirmed people lived."

"The ghosts didn't feel threatened?" Joel asked.

"Well, it maybe makes a small amount of sense, don't you think?" Kevin asked and grinned when he heard one of the locks give. "I told you I could do this," he bragged, starting on the second lock.

"You realize dude, that if we follow your line of reasoning," Stephen interjected, "the doctors and nurses would not have been among those infirmed and we don't know if anything ever happened to them. They could have been made to hurt themselves or got hurt. And we may not be safe if we go in there? I mean, we ain't exactly old or feeble either and *something* nailed you two in the head with your beer cans."

"Are you ever going to lay off that?" Joey griped.

"Maybe. Maybe not," Stephen grinned.

"You're probably right, Stephen. It was likely the ghostly grounds keeper pissed at our littering," Kevin concurred with a grin, but Joey didn't smile. "Come on, really? It's just a theory. There's absolutely nothing to support it. We don't have a clue who assaulted us with our own cans." Another lock opened, and Kevin set about working on the third, "Besides, guys, we can't have been the only people to come up here in the past fifteen years, and if anyone had been injured or gone missing, it would have made the news faster than a brush fire burning a dry field, don't ya think?

"I sure as hell hope you're right," Joey murmured, stepping into the foyer as Kevin popped the third lock and opened the door, "because my intentions today are to become rich and famous, not some dead person's scapegoat for retribution."

TWELVE

"I can't believe I'm actually back here. I haven't been here since I was a child," Mandy whispered, her mind drifting to the last time she and her mother had made this drive for the final time.

"I can't believe you bought the place, especially after the rumors that circulated about what happened to those three men back in ninety-three," Her fiancé, Parker Wentworth, interjected from the passenger seat.

Mandy laughed, "Don't tell me I'm marrying a man who won't purchase a place because a death occurred there."

"Deaths. Plural. And those are just the ones known of, associated with this place. For all we know, owning this property could invite death."

"Seriously?" Mandy laughed louder. "Oh Parker, you are such a goose."

"Are you saying that the deaths of those college boys—"

"I knew one of those guys…well, when he was a boy," Mandy inserted. "His eldest sister and I went to the same University together, and after my mother passed, she'd invite me to her home for the holidays, so I'd somewhere to go. I found myself spending quite a lot of time with them. They had a huge family, and Joey was the youngest of their litter. Joey and his two friends were always trying to find a reason to hang around me and Anne," Mandy snickered at the memory. "Anyway, I also found some comfort being near the place where I used to visit my grandmother regularly." Mandy Bartonelli eyed the monstrosity through the leafless autumn trees. Her newly purchased Jaguar made easy work of the rapidly ascending road, but she knew that if she wanted to visit the recently acquired property after this month, she'd need to rent a four-wheel drive vehicle, capable of plowing through the mounds of snow forecasted to layer the ground this winter.

"So, they ever actually link those rumors to the sanatorium?" Parker asked.

"Nope. All anyone recalls is that one of the guys told his parents that they were going to take a hike to the summit to see the place. Nobody knows if they actually came up here, and if they did, what happened. They just came up and never came back down—at least two of them didn't. Joey's sister relayed that, for months after their disappearance, the police combed the acreage around this facility and turned up zilch. There was even an attempt to search inside the premises, but the place was locked up tight…"

"Couldn't they have called the owner or the realtor to open the place up?"

"They could have, and maybe they did. I don't have all the facts. All I know is what Joey's sister told me. She said that the police decided the locks hadn't been tampered with, so jumped to the conclusion that they never entered the building. That left them with the assumption that something or someone attacked the men on their way up or down the mountain. Figured that one day, a hiker will stumble upon the bones."

"Dang, that's seriously messed up. You intimated that one guy survived?"

"Yeah. Joey," Mandy murmured, "if you'd call it surviving. He's messed up, big time. Living in a facility for the mentally challenged. Thing is, he claimed they got inside and were attacked by the residents of the place, but since the police couldn't find a way in, they determined that he'd just gone off his rocker."

"Seriously? You mean police didn't suspect this Joey of killing his two friends? Wouldn't that be more likely than believing his story that the poltergeists, did it?"

"I don't know the ins and outs. All I know is that they were barely even able to get two words out of Joey, so interrogating him over the purported deaths—"

"Purported? Two guys go missing, they aren't likely alive—"

"Since no bodies were ever found, and all they had were the ramblings of a messed-up college kid who could only sputter on about ghosts, they couldn't be certain the two missing didn't simply take off for Mexico."

"Without any justifiable reason…"

"Fear?" Mandy offered, interjecting. "Maybe they got so scared that they ran as far away as possible—"

"And their friend ended up in a nut house, completely off his gourd? I don't buy it. I think that this Joey got into a fight, killed 'em, left their bodies for the bears, then decided to make up the story about ghosts—"

"So, he could spend the remainder of his life in a house for the mentally insane. I don't think so."

"Or he didn't think that far ahead and ended up royally screwing himself. Act insane and get off but get locked away. He suddenly recovers, the police will be all over him again, looking for answers."

"I don't know, Parker. I sort of knew Joey, even though I'm nearly a decade older than he is, and I couldn't see him killing anybody, especially Stephen, his childhood friend, but I could see him getting the shit scared out of him and him ending up screwed in the head. He was kind of high strung, easily rattled."

"All right then, we'll say the place is haunted," Parker conceded, since their speculation wasn't getting the conversation anywhere. "So that brings me back to my original concern—if you know that it's a people-eating monster, why did you buy it? I mean, really Mandy, I researched the place inside and out when you laid the bombshell on me about wanting it, but I couldn't find anything that would justify spending nearly two million dollars, and after what we just discussed, it's supposedly haunted too?"

"No rumor about it, Parker. I happen to have it on good authority that the place is indeed haunted. That's one of the reasons I bought it. That's one of the reasons I don't think that Joey fabricated his story about his friends dying the way he said they did; although, I don't recall any other instances where the resident specters did anyone harm."

Parker gazed at Mandy oddly. "I've known you going on three years, Mandy, but I never took you for a ghost chaser. Is that why the weirdoes are following behind in the cliché white panel van?"

"Something like that," Mandy laughed, "Listen. I'm sorry I haven't divulged everything about my life to you, Parker, but I guess I thought if you knew everything there was to know about me and my family that you would...well...you'd hightail it in the opposite direction instead of marrying me. I do appreciate your coming along with me today though."

"You don't think I hired a private investigator to do a background check on you?" Parker said, wriggling his eyebrows absurdly. "Gotta guard my millions, you know?"

Mandy laughed, "No, actually I don't think you did, but if I'm wrong, then I'd prefer that you keep me forever in the dark about it."

"You got it," Parker laughed. "So, what made you buy it? Why the interest? Besides the fact that it's allegedly haunted?"

"Because I'm getting married," Mandy said softly in remembrance, "and once I change my last name, my family tree will wither and die."

"Okay, now you're just plain creeping me out."

Mandy laughed softly, "Sorry, honey. I'm not as weird as I sound."

"If I hadn't known you for the last three years as a perfectly sane, semi-intelligent woman, then I would be prone to disagree."

"Semi-intelligent?" Mandy huffed. "Keep it up, darling, and this car is going to be minus a passenger."

Parker laughed, "I'll stop if you promise to stop sounding creepy."

"I promise. Now, take the wallet out of my purse, will you?"

Parker leaned down and flipped the latch on the top of Mandy's Gucci purse, "Wow! I can't believe I'm being allowed into the sanctum walletus."

"Very funny, Parker! Just open the wallet, will you?"

Parker pulled the strap and opened the wallet. Two photos fell out onto his lap. "Who're they? Relatives of yours?"

"Yeah. The picture of the elderly woman is my grandmother, Rebecca Bartonelli. I called her Grannie Becca. The other is my grand aunt, Maria Bartonelli."

"Since I've never met them, can I assume that they are...well...dearly departed?"

"Maria died in October of nineteen twenty-seven—I was told, but we're not really certain. My grandmother died in October of nineteen seventy-three, just one month after my last visit to her here."

"Geez, I'm sorry to hear that," Parker said sincerely. "Is your grandmother the one who told you that the place was haunted?"

"Yes, but she really didn't have to," Mandy explained, taking the final bend in the road. "You see, the last time we were here, my mother saw a ghost. The next month, my grandmother died, and we never returned. I promised my grandmother...well, myself really, but it was a promise meant for my grandmother...anyway, I promised that, when I was old enough, I'd find a way to buy this place and tear it down. Somehow, in my child's mind, it was the ghosts that killed my Aunt Maria and Grannie Becca. I know that doesn't make sense, because my grandmother never said anything negative about her encounters, but I still associated it's being haunted with their deaths."

Parker was surprised to hear the vehemence in his fiancé's tone, "Your own mother passed away almost eight years ago in an auto accident. What took you so long to buy it if you were that determined? As sole heir to the Bartonelli fortune, it wasn't as if you had a long wait for the probate courts to release the money to you."

"A couple of reasons. Firstly, I wasn't that child anymore, so my determination to blame the spirits dissipated. I still wanted to buy it because of the connection to my relations, but not for the same reasons as when I was little. Secondly, I did look into it, but it wasn't available, and the owner refused to part with it then. It took a long time for him to finally decide to let it go, and when it came on the market, I made certain I got it."

"What made him decide to sell it finally? You'd think that, after sinking all that money into it to turning it into a geriatric facility—"

"Government shut that down long ago," Mandy interjected in a sharp tone. "Unsanitary conditions. Anyway, all I want to do now is assure myself that my grandmother's spirit isn't still lingering here before I have the place demolished; or the spirit of Maria Bartonelli."

"Hence the Ghostbusters back there?"

Mandy laughed, "Hence the Ghostbusters, but don't let them hear you call them that. They prefer to be called Specter Detectors. That's the name of the firm."

Parker laughed, "You've got to be kidding me! Specter Detectors? They'd have done better sticking with Ghostbusters."

Mandy parked the car and turned to face her fiancé, "Infringement or copyright issues, I'm sure. And don't crack any jokes, okay? I need these guys for my own piece of mind."

"Okay, sweetheart," Parker said, stroking her cheek. "I'll keep my tongue firmly in check."

"Thanks, darling." Mandy leaned over and gave him a swift kiss. "Well, let's get this show started." She opened the door and stepped out, quickly buttoning her jacket as a cold wind blew in from the ocean. She turned and looked back at the road, but the Spector Detectors weren't in view yet. "Let's get back in the car and wait. It looks as if their van is making the ascent a lot slower than my car did, and it's too cold to stand outside waiting."

"No argument from me. It feels like we should be in northern Alaska!" Parker exclaimed, echoing Mandy's thoughts. When they were back inside the car, Parker looked out from his window at the ruinous conditions of the building his fiancé recently purchased, "Kind of run down, isn't it?"

"Yeah. Doctor Markus, the prior owner, wanted to tear it down and build condos or something, that's why he wouldn't sell it initially, but the city declared it an historic landmark, so he couldn't. He held onto the property in the hopes that the restrictions would be lifted and petitioned them annually to do so, from what my attorney told me. When the city council refused, he opened it up to vandals in the hopes of making the powers that be change their minds."

"This place is an historic landmark? Really?"

Mandy laughed, "Not likely. It's more likely that the locals earned an income based on the rumors surrounding it being haunted, and to keep it from being torn down, and therefore impacting the local economy, the city council attached the historic landmark moniker to it."

"So, you bought a worthless building for two million dollars? I thought you bought it to tear it down too. So how are you going to get around that particular sanction?"

"They took the restrictions off the place in the Spring because interest in visiting saw a yearly decline after the disappearance of Joey's friends seven years ago. Their economy was impacted enough that when I broached the subject just after buying it, they barely hesitated. I guess they determined that if I am able to do something with it, it will inject the town with a new source of revenue."

"I'll bet that made the prior owner doubly pissed, especially since he could have, potentially, made something of it too."

"Guess the economy wasn't hurting bad enough yet for the council to change their minds. Dr. Markus did take the sell back to his attorney soon after they lifted the restrictions though. Hoping to find a loophole that he could take advantage of to void it, and even though my attorney assured me that the sale was iron-clad, we were still inundated with paperwork. Everything from claims of selling under duress to underhandedness—"

"What?"

"Yeah, he tried to prove that it was me who dissuaded the city council to not lift the restrictions; that I'd used coercion or bribery. That it was too coincidental that the council lifted the restrictions within months of my purchasing it. That's why it took all these months for me to get back up here. Both parties were forbidden access until all the legal issues were resolved. I'm just glad my attorney was better than his and finally filed an injunction preventing Markus's attorney from filing any more frivolous claims."

"I'm still trying to decide why this place is so valuable—"

"It's not. Remember, he wanted to tear it down to build condos. It's the land that's valuable. And had he been able to build what he wanted…well *that* would have been a gold mine."

"So, what are you going to build in its stead?"

"Condos," Mandy laughed. She spied the van topping the hill in her rearview mirror, blue smoke issuing from the tail pipe. The age and elevation had taken it toil on the old van so much so that she was surprised it even made the trek without breaking down. Still, she was glad it did. "Looks like it's time to get going. They've arrived." Mandy stepped out of the warmth of the car and immediately snuggled further into her coat. Parker was right about the frigidity. If she were going to build habitable dwellings, she'd have to do more to combat the wintry winds. There were trees lining the cliffs, but they were insufficient as a deterrent. "I could always make it a summer getaway spot," she muttered to herself.

The van crawled to a stop and the three Spector Detectors climbed out. Mandy walked over to greet Aries, leader of the Specter Detectors. "What do you think of the place?"

"Creepy, and definitely haunted. Star is already picking up some serious vibes. Are you sure that only two or three ghosts were seen here? Because the last time Star had a fit like this over a place, it was major-league infested."

"The doctor who bought the place claimed to have seen a ghost just before he purchased it and a few years after that, but that would have been in the mid-sixties. Then my mother fainted after she encountered a ghost, which would have been in the early seventies. And then there is my grandmother. She was a resident here for many years and says she conversed on a regular basis with Maria Bartonelli, a family member, who died here in the twenties—so she says."

"I thought you believed her?" Parker asked, confused.

"Not that I don't believe her, as such. I already explained that I do—sort of. It's just that my mother thought she was just lonely, so she made up an imaginary friend or that she was more ill than she let on. She was only sixty-nine back in nineteen seventy-three and put on a good show for my mother about being 'spry as a spring chicken', which she was, most days; but the autopsy revealed that she died from Meningococcal Disease, which she must have contracted shortly before or after our visit. Mother said that it was the meningitis that caused her to believe she was conversing with ghosts. A lot of the patients died that month from meningitis, not just my grandmother. It was one of the reasons why the long arm of the federal government stepped in and shut the place down."

"Dear sweet Jesus, Mandy. How did you and your mother get out of there without contracting it also? Meningitis is serious business!"

"I don't know, to be honest, and believe you me, my mother and I thanked our lucky stars more than once over the years that we were spared that fate. Anyway, even though I believe my grandmother believed what she said, there are people who contradict her accounts, say it's impossible she could have spoken to my grand aunt Maria. Before my father died, he told me that Maria was killed in an automobile accident—in New York. So, if that's the case, then how could she be haunting a deserted elderly home in California?"

"Well, if she was here, and your grandmother truly conversed with her on a regular basis," Aries said, following his crew toward the entrance, "then perhaps we'll pick up some trace of her along with your grandmother."

"Think I'll be able to talk to her at the same time as Grandmother Becca?" Mandy asked, following. "I mean, if she didn't die in an auto accident, it will be nice to know how she really died."

"Didn't your grandmother have a theory on that after talking to her? If she conversed with her so often, certainly her cause of death would not be a mystery," Parker said, tugging his jacket tighter around his ears as a gust of wind threatened to undress him. He picked up his pace, pulling Mandy along with him.

"If Maria revealed her cause of death, Grandma Becca didn't seem inclined to part with that particular information, but she was very convincing in her belief that Maria was a resident of this place in the late twenties." Mandy stopped before the massive door and pulled the keys from her purse. Her hands were frigid and shaking by the time she managed to locate a key and insert it into the first padlock. She worked diligently but continued conversing to keep her mind off the cold. "So, what Grandma Bekka did tell me was that my great-grandfather, Arthur Bartonelli shipped Maria here against her will from her home in Chicago because of something tragic that occurred in the family."

"But I didn't think that Dr. Markus opened the place to the elderly until the sixties." Parker moved further into the doorway in order to shield himself from the continuing brisk wind. The people from the Specter Detectors were not so fortunate, ducking behind each other and blowing warm breath into their shirts and hands while they paced back and forth in eager anticipation of getting inside to find shelter from the blustery winds.

"He didn't. Maria Bartonelli was here when it was a governmental facility for the mentally insane, in the twenties. Remember, I told you that?" Mandy asked, finding, and inserting the second key.

"Oh! That's right. It's just hard to keep the history of this place straight, not to mention your family tree, since the branches are all crooked." Parker said, rolling his eyes.

"More than you know," Mandy laughed.

"Hey, wait a minute," Parker exclaimed, "didn't you say at one point that the twenties were when they housed Tuberculosis patients in this facility?"

"That's correct," Mandy confirmed, "along with patients with mental illness."

"That doesn't seem safe. I mean, other than being a little sick in the head, wouldn't housing them in the same facility as those with tuberculosis put them at serious risk of contracting TB too?"

"Yeah, I'm not certain that some people didn't get TB, although they were housed on different floors. Even though I know quite a bit about the history of this place, I don't know everything."

"Maybe you can ask one of your relatives to fill in the blanks…if you ever get this place open," Parker complained.

"Locks are just a little old and frozen to boot. Shouldn't take…" The lock gave way. Mandy opened the door, and everyone started filing in quickly.

"That wind is killer," Aries observed, bringing up the rear. "It's a wonder anyone survived one winter in this place."

"It did have heat, you know," John quipped, lowering his equipment.

"You'd never know it by the temperature right now," Star added, still shivering. "What's it now, like ten degrees in here?"

"Closer to forty, I'd wager," Parker amended, "which is a hell of a lot better than the frigid ten degrees outside."

"Below twenty with the wind chill, is what it feels like," Aries whined, then shifted back to his professional state. "So, Miss Bartonelli, this is your show. Where do you want us to start?"

"Mandy?" Parker placed a hand on his fiancé's arm when she did not respond to Aries' question. "Are you okay, babe?"

"Yeah, sure," Mandy whispered, a catch in her throat. "It's just that I'm coming to terms with the fact that I haven't stepped inside this place in twenty-seven years. I don't see how I could have missed the horrible conditions my grandmother endured living here, or how my mother could have kept her here all those years. This place is wretched."

"Sweetheart, I'm sure it was a lot nicer back in the sixties and seventies. You've got to remember that this place has been deserted for about twenty years," Parker comforted.

Mandy nodded, wiping a stray tear from her eye, "Aries, I want to poke around down here for a bit, if you want to try to get some readings from the children's ward. There's been a rumor for a decade about a little boy named Jimmy, a tuberculosis patient, who loves to play ball with the visitors—with what visitors there used to be. Might be good for you since he could be quite lonely by now and eager for a little play time."

"What about the fifth floor?" Aries asked. "Isn't that where your grandmother and grand aunt resided? Thought you wanted us to do a séance, see if anything pops."

"I do, but I want to snoop around down here for a little while, so

I thought you guys might like to take some readings, or whatever it is you do."

"Sounds good. What floor was the children's ward on?"

"Sixth floor."

"Um, Mandy," Star began tentatively, a shiver running along her spine, "you haven't by chance heard the rumors circulating that the poltergeists on the fourth and fifth floors are less than inviting, have you? Are you sure you want to set up the séance on one of those floors?"

"A lot of bad things took place on those particular floors," John added, "which would probably make the ghosts there less than friendly."

"I haven't heard anything that would suggest anyone was ever harmed—" Mandy started.

"Except the three college kids," Parker interjected.

"Right, but that's unsubstantiated," Mandy replied. "So, what rumors have I missed, Star? What have you heard about the fourth and fifth floors?"

Aries answered for her, "Certainly you've heard about the experiments that took place on the TB and mental patients here. Lobotomies and other experimental brain surgeries resulting in the untimely deaths of hundreds of patients?"

"I am aware, yes, but all of the information I've gathered suggests that any ghosts are benign—"

"Except for Joey's account," Parker interjected again.

Mandy sighed heavily, "Parker, I love you dearly, but you need to stop now. I am fully aware of the *one* account that alludes to the entities abiding here being unfriendly, but that's one account. I'm asking if there are other rumors that I haven't been made privy to."

Star stared up the stairwell, a distant look in her eyes, "We aren't welcomed here," she murmured, and Mandy sighed again.

"Okay," Mandy said, her tone frustrated, "Let's just say that the ghosts over the last two decades have gotten suddenly cranky. Either way, I'm not here to disturb them, I'm simply here to converse with my relatives. So, on your way up to meet Jimmy, maybe you can let them know that's our intent, Star."

"I've heard that there have been quite a few people who've made their way up here over the last couple of decades that were never heard from again," John asserted.

"Really? Where did you hear that, because I've not heard anything of the kind," Mandy insisted, trying to quash all of the nonsense talk that would serve no purpose but to set all of them on their toes. "I understand being nervous about being here, but I thought this is what you guys did? Search out ghosts and perform séances and stuff. Are you saying you don't want to go through with it now that you've seen the place?"

"We know it's creepy," Parker added, "Hell, the place scares the pants off of me, so we'll understand if you want to back out. But you know that we can't pay you if you don't stay."

Aries nodded, and then jerked his head to the side, motioning for his crew to follow him. Apparently, a conference was in order. Mandy watched the three confer in the corner, John nodding and Star shaking her head. It was obvious that not all three were united in their opinions. When they returned, Mandy knew that Star had been outvoted—they were staying. Star looked none-too-happy, staring around at the walls and ceiling in trepidation.

"We'll be heading up to the sixth floor now," Aries stated firmly, heading towards the elevator.

"I'd recommend taking the stairs," Mandy said, halting their progress. "That elevator's has been out of use for over twenty years, so I can't attest to its reliability. Wouldn't want anyone getting stuck in there."

The three paranormal detectives turned in unison and headed for the staircase. "Give a shout when you're ready to begin our work on the fifth floor," Aries said.

"How about we meet there in an hour?" Parker said.

Aries nodded, then turned to address his people, "Okay, guys. Let's go see if Jimmy wants to play some ball games.

THIRTEEN

"So, do you really think you'll find these supposed lost records, Mandy?" Parker asked, after Aries and his crew disappeared inside the door to the stairwell. "That *is* the reason you wanted to stay down here and snoop about for a while, isn't it?"

Mandy nodded, making her way down the hallway.

"Come on, Mandy, that's a rumor that's floated about since the thirties from what you've told me, and just as non-provable as the existence of the ghosts residing here. And even if there were records, don't you think the prior owners would have found them long ago?"

"Not if they weren't looking for them," Mandy asserted, stopping at the door to the records room. "Just because they couldn't find proof of illegally held mental patients, doesn't mean I won't."

"Okay, let's say for argument's sake, that there were people held here against their will in the twenties, do you think they would dare to keep a file on those people? And, even if they did have files, what good could come of finding them now?"

"I did my research, and the doctor in charge in the twenties—Doctor Santanini—was a government employee," Mandy persisted, pulling her ring of keys from her purse.

"And what does that have to do with the price of corn in China?"

"Haven't you ever noticed that the government has a fetish for keeping records and files on every little thing?" Mandy asked, sorting through her ring of keys. She found the one she was searching for and slid it into the rusted lock. It squealed in protest, but finally gave way with a pop. Mandy pushed the door open, returned the ring of keys to her purse, and pulled out her flashlight. "Without records, they couldn't get funded, couldn't receive required medications," she concluded finally.

"Again, I repeat my previous question." Parker stepped into the darkened office. He shone the beam from his flashlight around the room. "It would be nice if the electricity was working."

Mandy laughed, "You'd have never made it living a hundred years ago."

"Never get an argument from me on that, so what does the government have to do with this search?"

"Check for loose or out-of-place flooring," Mandy said, aiming her light at the floor. "As for being a government employee, he would have kept records, as the government does on everything. Records that the government doesn't want the general public to see, however—"

"Is censored to the point of being non-readable?"

"Redacted, you mean? Or stashed away from other files," Mandy amended, laughing. "Anyway, my research indicated that Doctor Santanini died late in his tenure, after the date that I was given for my grand aunt Maria's passing, which means any files he may have started on her, or other patients residing here secretly, may still be hidden somewhere in this or another office."

"Patient records of those people who weren't *meant* to be here and you're hoping to find evidence that supports your belief that your grandmother wasn't hallucinating when she said she spent hours talking to your grand aunt? Aren't you reaching a bit, Mandy? How will records prove your grandmother actually spoke with your grand aunt and why does it matter now?"

"I guess I'll just feel better knowing I searched. I know that even if we managed to find any files, there isn't anyone still alive to hold accountable; but just being able to counter my father's accounts and to substantiate my grandmothers would bring me a modicum of peace. If I don't find anything here, maybe a séance will reveal how my grand aunt really died."

"You don't believe your father then?"

"I can't explain why. It seems a plausible explanation, passed down from my great grandfather, so technically, I don't believe my great grandfather. Still, Maria could very well have died as he said. There are simply too many things telling me that my great grandfather's story was fabricated."

"Such as?" Parker tapped his heel along the floorboards, searching for any that may hold the answers his fiancé sought.

"Well," Mandy continued, tapping floorboards on the other side of the room. "It was the 1920s, right?"

"Okay, and?"

"And my family lived in Chicago, so what would my grand aunt Maria be doing in New York—driving! Everything I know about the 1920s indicate that women rarely traveled alone, not to mention drove? And if a woman came from a family such as mine, where the men are obsessive over their women, the likelihood of her being in New York, alone, driving, diminishes to near zero possibility."

"Okay, plausible. And honestly it sounds as if you've already made up your mind that the reason given about her death was a lie, so I guess I'm just trying to decide why this means so much to you—still. It isn't as if you knew her, right?"

Mandy stopped tapping floorboards and plopped down on her butt, sighing heavily, "My grandmother was convinced that Maria was here; that she spoke to Maria's spirit many times. So, if my great grandfather's explanation is true, that would make my grandmother go nuts; and I cannot abide thinking that. I *did* know her, and she wasn't crazy. If I can find the truth about my grand aunt's whereabouts and how she died, it would vindicate my grandmother and provide me some closure also, I suppose. Yes, I'm as certain as can be that my great-grandfather lied about how Maria died, but she could have died elsewhere in a different manner. To discover records would settle all doubt."

"But most important is to prove your grandmother wasn't senile?"

"Yeah," Mandy replied softly.

"Because if she's proven mentally incompetent postmortem, then what? You think that senility might run in your genes?" Parker asked, the light of understanding finally glowing bright in his brain. All this time, he'd assumed curiosity drove Mandy's quest for answers, but now he knew that the reasons went far deeper. Mandy nodded, her gaze lowered, confirming his inference. Parker walked over and sat down next to her, placing his arm in comfort about her shoulder. "If it helps any, I know you pretty good, and even though I was worried you might have stepped off the deep end a few times during this pursuit of yours, I never thought you were completely cuckoo."

Mandy smiled softly, "Thanks. I think."

"You're welcome," he replied, placing a kiss on her cheek. "Let's finish stomping on some floors because we're supposed to meet up with the Spector Detectors in about twenty minutes. Now that's a group whose mental stability could truly come into question."

"Stop picking on them," Mandy chastised lightly, standing, and brushing off her jeans.

"I wonder how they're getting on with Jimmy?" Parker asked when he heard a squeal reverberate down the stairwell.

"Sounds like he may have startled them." Mandy grinned. "Come on, let's keep searching."

FOURTEEN

Despite her fear of the place, Star was entranced.

She watched the ball circle around a central point slowly, and then roll behind John over to a nearby window. Each could have explained it all away logically, had they been inclined to be logical. For instance, had there been grooves in the wooden floor in which the ball could follow, they may be shaking their heads in disappointment rather than bemusement. None cared for logic at present, for all three were too busy engaging in a game of ball with specter boy to feel anything but awe.

When it came to past ghostly encounters, they had little illusion that logic, reason, or even science prevailed over the paranormal. Old pipes groaning, rats thumping beneath floorboards and behind wall panels, wind whistling through cracks in window mountings, all provided logical explanations, debunking nearly all potential hauntings. Even their EVP sessions convinced them of nothing more than the existence of power of persuasion and auditory illusion. Star, the gifted one, never really felt evidence of the supernatural. Of course, they didn't tell their clients of their disillusionment. They needed a paycheck as much as the next guy; however, they generally knew the real deal because Star possessed a genuine gift. If they entered a building in which spirits still resided, Star knew it. Of course, that had only happened once and was very innocuous. Still, neither Aries nor John doubted her gift. She was also a gifted actress, because she knew how important a paycheck was too; so, if someone hired them to check out a building and Star registered nothing...well, they could still convince the owner of a severe infestation and even perform a convincing séance or two.

That wasn't a worry here. Star's reaction to the place was as real as was her fear of the place—a palpable fear, almost forgotten while they interacted with Jimmy.

"Do you think we have time to have a séance with Jimmy?" Star asked, watching the ball slowly make its way across the floor. Her feet prevented any further forward momentum.

John glanced at his watch, "Sure. We've only been here fifteen minutes. We don't need to meet up with the others for a while yet. Why don't we give it a try?"

Star smiled. It was her first genuine smile since entering the place, and that made John smile, "Set up here?" He asked.

"Absolutely," Star replied, enthusiastically. The ball, which had remained still next to her shoe, suddenly rolled with fervency in a straight line, and smacked the side of John's shoe. "Well, now would be a good time, since he's very active," Star smiled. "If we can get him to settle long enough to interact with more than the ball, that is." To Aries she said, "Don't bother setting up everything. We haven't the time. Just the EMF reading and the video camera."

Aries quickly retrieved the two items and set up, while Star continued rolling the ball to the space beneath the window, to a boy unseen. Once, during the five-minute wait, she'd rolled the ball in the opposite direction, which yielded no return—literally. She'd had to walk over to retrieve the ball, then rolled it again toward the window. Within a minute, it rolled back. That had myriad questions rolling about through Star's mind: Either there really was some distortion in the flooring, not visible to the naked eye, that ensured a return trip; or little Jimmy was disinterested or unable to engage in an area other than beneath that window. She really needed to know which. She had no doubt there was a presence in the room, but just what type of presence was the mystery. A little boy who loved games, or something other. Just then, Aries announced all was ready, so Star sat down on the floor in the center of the room. The ball rolled from beneath the window and stopped at her legs. She touched it but didn't roll it back.

"Jimmy," she said softly. "I know you like to play, but can you reveal yourself to me? No harm will come to you, I promise."

Aries shook his head, revealing no alterations in the EMF.

Star looked at John, "He's here. I know he's here; or someone is," she whispered. John nodded.

"If this isn't Jimmy, perhaps we've been playing ball with someone else," Star tried. "I would truly love to know with who. Tell me your name?"

Aries' eyes widened, but he remained silent. He nodded. The EMF was reading something. In all the time he'd been with the Spector Detectors, this was the first genuine reading he'd ever saw, and he didn't know how to react. John had told him that Star was genuinely gifted, could genuinely sense the presence of those who'd passed on; but although he was fascinated by the prospect of encountering a ghost, he never truly thought he ever would. He was also so used to putting a show on for their clients, he didn't know what was real anymore. He'd often wondered whether Star even believed anymore.

"Someone else then," Star whispered, fascinated. "A friend of Jimmy's perhaps?"

Aries shook his head, and Star sighed, "Okay, not a friend, but someone who definitely loves to play ball." Aries nodded and Star continued, "If you want me to roll the ball back to you, I'd prefer to see you first. I wouldn't want to roll it the wrong way."

Aries again shook his head and Star sighed again, heavily, "It doesn't matter, you can put the gear away. He's gone."

"It's as though he doesn't want anyone trying to talk to him. Playing is fine, but not communicating," Aries added, slowly turning, panning his video lens around the room, from ceiling to floor. "I'll put the gear away in a minute. I just want footage of the room. Never know if we might capture something—for real this time."

"Since we have a few minutes," John suggested, "why don't we make our way down to the fifth floor and start setting up. Room *502*, wasn't it?" He bent to retrieve his own gear.

"Yeah, sounds good," Aries stopped recording, and started packing up. Within a minute, both men headed for the hallway, stopping when they realized that Star wasn't following.

"If the thought of going to the fifth floor is too much for you, Star, you can stay here and play with Jimmy, or whoever it is. We could use you in there though, ya know? You're the one with the actual psychic gift. All we know how to do is affect pretense," Aries tone was sympathetic and soothing.

"If I go down there, I know I will feel so much pain and suffering. I can feel the residuals of it here, just standing a floor above," Star whispered, her distress reverberating around the small room. "I could sense the horror and anguish drifting down the stairwell when we first entered—the torment of those unfortunates residing on the fifth floor, and the pain of those from the fourth floor."

Aries glanced at John, worry in his eyes. He'd never seen Star behave like this. John shrugged his shoulders, answering Aries unasked question—no, he'd never seen her like this before either. Aries turned back to face Star. She was staring down at the ball still nestled against her shoes. He started to speak, but no sound came. At least no sound registered in Star's ears. She had blocked out all sounds now, her focus on the ball too intent to allow intrusion.

An atom bomb could explode next to her, and she wouldn't budge. Tears filled her eyes as she locked gazes with the ghost of a little boy, sitting cross-legged next to the ball, but what startled her even more was that he'd returned, and she hadn't sensed it. That made her wonder whether she could always sense the presence of a spirit, or if she only could when they permitted it. That left her feeling shaken, because if she couldn't sense every presence on the fourth and fifth floor, there could be entities there waiting to do them harm, and she'd have no forewarning. She drew in a deep breath and shook the thought away.

With care, she slowly settled on the floor across from the little boy, crossing her legs in like fashion. She smiled tentatively and was pleased to see him respond in kind.

"Hello," she said softly, "I'm Star."

Aries and John immediately ceased speaking. It was showtime. With motions exaggeratedly slow, they lifted their video cameras and punched 'record'.

"Can you tell me your name?" Star asked, cautious to remain still. She didn't want to startle him.

"Sebastian," came the echo-y reply.

"Hello, Sebastian," Star smiled widely, drawing in a deep breath of joy. "Are you the one who really likes to play ball up here?"

The spectral image nodded, and Star smiled widely, knowing now that the stories of Jimmy could have been fabricated to up the allure of the place. Still, she wondered—

"Do you know a boy named Jimmy?" She asked and knew her speculation had been correct, for Sebastian shook his head.

"Why did you stop playing with me?" The boy asked.

Star smiled encouragingly, "I thought you'd left, so I was going to explore the other rooms. Do you play with everyone who comes here?"

Sebastian shook his head, "People who come don't want to play with me," he replied sadly.

"But you've tried to play with them," Star stated, seeking confirmation of prior engagement.

Sebastian nodded, "They just squeal or scream or watch the ball roll. They don't really want to play. You want to play though, don't you?"

Star nodded, "I do. I have other places to go to first, but I would love to come back and play with you again. Would that be okay?"

The boy lowered his head and vanished. He was gone again.

FIFTEEN

Star looked at peace. She closed her eyes and breathed, deeply and steadily. She'd also stopped her seemingly one-sided conversation, which was their cue that she'd ended her ghostly encounter. Prior times, her affectation was a ruse, but there was something different this time, and they knew it. They made their way over to where she still sat cross-legged and settled on their haunches next to her.

"How did it go?" Aries asked quietly, his tone almost reverent.

Star smiled. "Sebastian is lonely."

"Sebastian? Not Jimmy?" Aries asked. Although they'd heard her speaking, not everything had come across clearly because she spoke in so low a whisper.

"Not Jimmy," Star confirmed.

"Did you get any satisfactory answers to your questions?" John asked.

"To some, yes, but he went away before I could ask him more questions. He seemed disappointed that I needed to stop playing with him for a while."

"How old would you say he was?" John asked.

"About five or six years of age. He looked sickly," Star said sadly.

"The tuberculosis, most likely," Aries supplied.

"I didn't hear you ask about the fourth or fifth floor, but did he say anything about that?" John queried.

Star shook her head, wiping the dust from her jeans. "He was only interested in my staying to play with him. He seemed so lonely, the poor darling."

"Are you sure you aren't just transferring some of your own insecurities onto his reactions?" John asked, shouldering his video camera.

Star shrugged, "There's always a risk of that happening I suppose but I don't think so this time. The look of sadness on his face was genuine enough, and he just kept mentioning that he wanted to play. Are we still going to set up in room *502*?" She asked, glancing at her watch. "It's nearly time to meet up with our clients." There was a reticence in her tone that John and Aries picked up on. She was putting on a front of bravery but couldn't hide her fear—not altogether.

"It's what we're getting paid for Star," Aries said firmly. "Like I said, we could use you in there, but will wing it if we have to."

"Okay," Star acquiesced. "Hopefully the ghosts in that particular room will be as friendly and accommodating as Sebastian was."

"Fingers crossed," John grinned.

Star smiled in reply, but she knew that those they were likely to encounter were not going to be friendly and accommodating, not if her sense about those who'd occupied those floors were correct. Her mind drifted to Amanda Bartonelli, who was convinced that nothing untoward had ever happened to anyone at this establishment, but if that was true, then why was every nerve in her brain firing a warning to stay away?

SIXTEEN

"Well, we've tapped on and torn up nearly every floorboard in every room down here, with no results, other than to give the demolition team a head start," Parker quipped.

Mandy sighed, and wiped a dusty arm against her sweaty forehead, "Okay, I will concede that perhaps we are not likely to find any hidden files. Damn!"

"Hey, that doesn't necessarily mean the rumors weren't true, just perhaps that Doctor Santanini broke governmental protocol and destroyed any proof of illegally held patients; or his successor…what was his name? The guy that opened the geriatric facility?"

"Dr. Markus."

"Right, or Dr. Markus located them during his renovations of the place." Parker glanced at his watch, "It's about time for us to join your Specter Detectors, so maybe they can commune with one of your relatives and get the answers you're looking for."

Mandy shook her head, disappointment etched on her face. "I guess I was just hoping to find tangible proof that Amanda Bartonelli didn't die in an automobile accident in New York, or anywhere else but here; provide vindication that Grandma Becca wasn't a fruitcake."

"I get why you want to know, sweetheart—now. I'm not sure I wouldn't want to know if it were someone in my family. I mean, you've got conflicting accounts of how a family member died. That alone can be aggravating, but to have doubts cast on the mental stability of one beloved, I get that, I do, but you've done all you can to locate any records pertaining to your grand aunt, so let's see if the psychics you hired can't put some of your questions to rest, okay? That is why you brought them, yeah? So, chin up," Parker looked into his fiancé's troubled gaze, glistening with tears, "and let's see what the séance reveals. There's a good chance that both Rebecca and Maria Bartonelli will provide all sorts of sordid details about your family history. More than you may want to know."

Or more than you'd want to know, she thought, but instead said, "You're right; of course, so let's head up...what the hell?" Mandy jerked at the loud noises drifting down from the upper floor.

"Sounds as if someone is throwing stuff against the walls. We'd better get up there." Parker took off toward the stairwell when another loud bang rent the air.

SEVENTEEN

Parker and Mandy hit the stairwell just as a louder thud reverberated through the walls.

"What is going on up there?" Mandy gasped, breathing short and labored from the cold as she raced up the stairs behind Parker. "It sounds like they're tossing their equipment against the walls."

"It's definitely not what I'd expect to be hearing, unless head-banging is part of their repertoire," Parker huffed, stopping suddenly at the fourth-floor landing.

"What's wrong?"

"Sounds like the noise is coming from the fifth floor, but didn't the Detectors say they were headed for the sixth-floor children's ward to play with Jimmy?"

Mandy nodded, then glanced at her watch, "This is the time we said we'd meet them, so the noise may be coming from them. And wouldn't we hear them coming down from the sixth floor if they'd heard the same banging we did? We've certainly made a ruckus dashing up here to check it out. I doubt that three people barreling down the stairs would be a silent event."

Parker nodded, then started up the final flight of stairs to the fifth floor, "I hope, admittedly, that head-banging is a part of their set-up process, because the alternative doesn't make my belly feel very good."

"Mine either."

Parker yanked at the door to the fifth-floor landing, and immediately fell backwards, bumping into Mandy who was right behind him.

"Hey! Careful! I just finished climbing these and don't particularly want to start over. What's with you?"

Parker wiped a thick layer of sweat from his brow and then turned to face Mandy, "The doorknob is scorching hot. Like a pot handle that's conducted too much heat from the stove."

"I don't understand," Mandy eyed her fiancé's flushed skin with concern. "There's no heat in this building."

"There is on this floor." He stepped back up to the door, pulling his coat over his hand. He gripped the doorknob and gave it a quick turn, then pushed the door open a crack. With a startled cry, he stepped back again. "Son of a bitch!"

"What? What's wrong?" Her fear elevated as the noises of things being hurled around grew louder.

"You can't feel that heat escaping from the opening? Stick your hand through there." He stepped aside, so Mandy could sidle past him.

Mandy eyed him quizzically, then stepped forward and slid her hand through the small opening. "Ow!" She cried, yanking her hand back.

"Like I said—scorching hot," Parker ran a hand through his hair nervously, and leaned against the stairwell railing, continuing to run his hands through his hair in thought.

Thud after thud continued pounding against the walls, but they heard not a sound from the Specter Detectors. "Do you think they're in there?" Mandy paced up and down the first few steps, her arms crossed worriedly across her chest. "The Spector Detectors?"

"Do *you* think they're in there?"

"I don't know. They certainly aren't here with us trying to figure out what's going on in there?"

"Maybe the noise didn't reach them on the fifth floor—" Parker started, then started cursing up a blue streak beneath his breath, knowing that was unlikely.

"If they *are* in one of the rooms on that hallway, what's that banging noise, and why it is so hot in there?" Mandy asked rhetorically. Just then, a female scream rent the air, causing Parker and Mandy to leap back down the stairwell. They stopped at the fourth-floor landing, their breaths coming in huge gasps.

"Oh my God, they are there," Mandy cried. "Do you think they're okay?"

"Do *you* really think that scream sounded joyous? Look, with that heat, they'll be blistered, without a doubt, but if they don't get out of there soon, they're going to look like the charcoal briquettes after a barbeque." Parker headed back up the steps.

"What are you going to do?"

"I don't know what we can do, but if we can at least get a look into the corridor." Parker took a step back, lifted his leg, and slammed his foot into the door. It banged open, the rusted hinges jamming as it smashed into the wall. He stepped to the boundary between cold and hot, easily discernible by the red hue close to the ground. There was also a perceptible distortion in the air as heat rising from a desert roadway. It was as if an undetectable heating element ran lengthways down the hall. He peered as far down the corridor as possible, "What are their names again?"

"Aries is the boss, and there's Star and John."

"John! Can you hear me, man?"

"Dear Lord, above," Mandy whispered as the heat dissipated instantaneously. Hesitantly, she took a step into the corridor and then looked back at Parker, a look of near horror etched on his face. "It's as if someone simply flicked a switch," she whispered.

"Yeah, well, they can easily switch it back on, so do you mind stepping back into the landing please?" Parker reached out and snagged Mandy's hand. He pulled her next to his side, then stuck his head through slowly, peering down the corridor in both directions, "I don't see anything, and we can put to rest any doubts about the place being haunted. My only concern now is getting down the hall to check on the Ghostbusters. If that was Star that we heard scream."

"Who else would it have been?

"A specter from the experimentation days here?" Parker asked. When Mandy looked at him incredulously, he sighed, "Okay, so, what'll we do?"

"The flooring looks strong enough to walk on," Mandy supplied, stepping gingerly back into the landing. "At least the flooring doesn't appear to have been affected by the heat. It's as if it never happened, but it did happen."

"That's my biggest concern, whether or not we'll make it down there and back *before* the ghosts decide to flick the heat back on and turn us into ash."

"Oh yeah, right!"

"John!" Parker yelled again. "Answer me!"

"Star! Aries!" Mandy joined, "Can anyone hear us?"

"I feel as if I'm in one of those b-rated horror movies," Parker said, rubbing a hand over his face in frustration, "and if we make a move to try to help them, some ghost with a sick sense of humor is going to re-ignite the corridor and we're going to get fried or something."

"Well, we certainly can't leave them in there," Mandy snapped. "What if they're hurt, or worse?"

"I'd wager on worse. Have you ever *watched* a horror movie, Mandy? Any time anyone dares to venture where they shouldn't, they end up ghost fodder, and no one ever finds their bodies, which is probably what happened to those two college men you mentioned from seven years ago. For all we know, their ashes fill the fibers of the faded carpet in one of the rooms lining this corridor."

"And you're psyching yourself out. This isn't a movie. This is real-life—unfortunately—and unfortunately, we have no choice but to go down that hall to see what's happened to Aries, Star, and John. In a way, they're our responsibility. After all, this *is* my property, and I *did* hire them."

"And if something has happened to them, you're opening yourself up to a humongous lawsuit," Parker finished. "Still, you're right. I've seen too many horror flicks, which is why I'm hesitant to step foot in that hallway."

"Yeah, but we need to try." Mandy moved back into the corridor, praying that whoever flipped the heat on the first time was done playing that particularly demented game. She glanced down the hallway and sucked in a low breath of dismay, "Oh, God," she hissed, "Parker! Look!"

Parker's gaze followed Mandy's pointing finger, "Dear Lord above!" He whispered in horror.

"That's it! We've got to get down there!" Without waiting to see if Parker was following, she bolted down the hallway toward one of the rooms from which protruded a blackened hand, clawing desperately at the carpeting; the only indication that anyone still lived.

EIGHTEEN

Mandy paced the corridor of Saint Peter's Memorial Hospital, her thoughts in turmoil. She glanced at her fiancé, sitting with his lowered head clasped in his hands, obviously as deep in disturbing thought as she.

She still could not get past the sight that met them when they reached that room. The only word her mind could conjure to process the sight was *ghastly*, but still, that could not describe it well enough. There was not a descriptive word in any language that could do justice to what she'd witnessed, unless one thought to apply the word *ghostly*.

It was Aries' hand they saw which had finally shaken the fear from them and spurred them into action, placing thoughts of their own safety aside. Yet the only way she'd been able to determine his identity was by the remains of an onyx ring that Aries wore on his left thumb. It was nearly as nondescript as the body, distorted and disfigured from the unbelievable heat that had engulfed the fifth floor.

The heat had twisted and deformed everything in the room—dissolved all into macabre distortions. Aries, Star and John included. If not for the bone, she and Parker would not have been able to distinguish body from furnishings. She couldn't help thinking that her and Parker's shouting had somehow caused the heat to be switched off, even if it was too late to save the three detectives. Even if the heat dissipated suddenly without any help from their calls…she shuddered again, for if the heat had remained on, the bones may have gone the way of the flesh—disintegrated into nothingness. She shuddered and fought the urge to run to the nearest restroom and empty the contents of her stomach into the toilet.

"Miss Bartonelli?" A voice said, pulling her thoughts back from her property to the morgue corridor. "Thank you for waiting."

"Sheriff?" At his nod, Mandy extended her hand, but her hand was limp, and her gaze glazed, as if the handshake was habit. "Thank you for coming," she continued in a flat tone that told him she was simply replying by rote rather than being cognizant of her words. He wondered if either were truly present or if they were still back at the scene of the crime.

"Who might you be, young man?" Joe asked, bending at the waist to attempt to get the man to engage, which he barely did.

"Parker Wentworth," he murmured with the same flat tone as had Mandy Bartonelli. He knew they were in shock, but he also knew he needed answers. Shock and interrogation never produced coherent results, in his experience, but that didn't stop him trying.

"Mr. Wentworth," the sheriff acknowledged. "So, if we're in a morgue then I expect you two have something to tell me that isn't exactly pleasant?"

"We didn't know who else to call," Parker whispered, looking up and responding as if just seeing the sheriff for the first time.

"Then calling the sheriff's department was the best thing you could do. You made the right call, especially as I'm to understand there's been an accident of some sort—"

"I'm not certain that homicide would fit," Parker murmured. "But I do think it was murder—I think."

"Whoa! Back up," the sheriff exclaimed, "and Miss Bartonelli, please sit. You look on the verge of collapse. Since we're in the morgue instead of the hospital upstairs, then there's been a death, so that much is clear. But now I'm hearing murder."

Mandy sniffed loudly and blew her nose as tears threatened to overwhelm her yet again. She settled on the bench beside Parker and took a deep breath, letting it out long and loud.

"Now, it's obvious you two have suffered a trauma, but I need you to keep with me until I can sort some things out, so perhaps you'd better tell me what's happened from the beginning."

"Maybe you should see for yourself, Sheriff," the medical examiner said, stepping through the swinging doors. "I don't think words could justify what was done to these poor people."

"Okay, Frank," the sheriff replied, glancing curiously at the two young people sitting shocked and silent on the bench. "I don't expect you two will be leaving?"

Both shook their heads and the sheriff nodded, "Okay, Frank, you have my attention. Show me what you've got."

"This way." Frank turned and pushed through the swinging doors leading to the autopsy room. "I would suggest you use this," he said, handing over some Vicks VapoRub, "and prepare yourself," he cautioned, pausing by one of the sheet-covered gurneys.

The sheriff stepped to the other side of the gurney, then nodded when he'd braced his willpower, "Go ahead."

Frank took a deep, steadying breath, and then pulled the sheet aside, exposing the overcooked, bony remains, bits and pieces of bloodied epidermis, blue jeans, and silky material still clinging throughout. The sheriff turned, shuddering. He'd seen carnage before, but this...

"It had the same effect on me, Joe," Frank said, "and I'm the medical examiner."

"Are the others the same?"

"Pretty much. The body's covered now if you want to turn around." Joe took a final breath and turned, looking at the sheet as if it might suddenly jump up and assault him.

"You look a bit pasty, Joe. Why don't you go out in the corridor with the other two, and I'll be out in a second."

"How?"

"I can't answer that. I'm a doctor, but to ascertain cause of death, I'm going to need to call in a forensic pathologist. Go on. I'll be out in a sec," the M.E. reiterated. "In the meantime, those two out there can probably provide some detail—"

"*They* didn't do this, did they?"

"I didn't say that, Joe. Besides that's not for me to determine. Still, if I had to hazard a guess, I can't see them causing this sort of damage and then hauling the bodies in here. Anyway, I said go talk to them. Your job, remember? Mine is to try to sort this mess…to get some help sorting out this mess. I'll call you back in if my preliminary turns up anything of interest."

Joe nodded, thinking just how big a mess this really was, but the biggest mess for Joe right now was to determine whether this was murder or manslaughter, and if it wasn't committed by one of the two sitting outside in the corridor, by whom was it committed, and how and why? He moved a bit unsteadily toward the swinging doors, glancing back over his shoulder once before pushing through. When the doors swung shut behind him, he stood for a moment, collecting his bearings, eyeing the two young people still sitting exactly as he'd left them moments before. Whatever had happened to the three people in the morgue had happened to these two as well, he surmised—only they'd survived to tell the tale.

NINETEEN

Joe stood watching the two young people for a few minutes more, trying to decide how best to proceed. He'd never encountered anything like this in his forty-plus years on the force and wished he had not done so now. He thought about hauling them down to the police station, but neither looked capable of more than sitting and quivering at present. How they managed to bring those bodies into the morgue was beyond his comprehension. It angered him a bit that they *had* hauled them here, because that meant his crime scene was already contaminated. Berating them wasn't going to change that though, neither would it get them to open up and answer needed questions. Treading lightly always worked better in these circumstances than beating someone over the head with a stick.

If they were not who he knew them to be, he'd have not a doubt that they somehow had a hand in this, but he did know at least one of them, knew of her family, and knew her to be a decent kid—even though her pedigree was questionable. In fact, because he did know her, he was extremely surprised that she had not yet summoned her attorney. The other young man he knew by name alone—if he were indeed related to the Wentworths of Wentworth Industries, which was likely if he'd attached himself to a Bartonelli. A lot of power and money in that union, which made him wonder why Wentworth's attorney wasn't here also. Why a team of attorneys weren't present and circling the wagon around their clients.

He brought his thoughts back, then went to speak to them again. "After what I've just seen," the sheriff began in the sympathetic tone he used to invoke a feeling of comfort. He pulled up a nearby folding metal chair and settled across from them, "I'm surprised that you two haven't completely lost your mind. I do have a question that's been kind of gnawing at me though since seeing them, besides the obvious one that is. Mind telling me how you managed to get those three bodies to the morgue without the local police finding out about it first?"

"We brought them," Parker croaked. A shudder raced along his spine, and he shivered as if a chill wind shot down the back of shirt and grazed his skin.

"Kind of figured that much, but it's the *how* part of the equation that I hadn't quite figured out yet."

"We found some sheets," Mandy whispered, sniffled, took a deep breath, and then released it with a bone-shaking shudder. "We couldn't just leave them there. The heat could have been switched back on at any moment. We put them in the back of their van and—" Mandy stopped, bringing her hands up to cover her face. She couldn't go on; could not relive the nightmare right now; maybe never again. If she thought she could pay to have her memory erased, like in some sci-fi adventure flick, she'd be there right now instead of sitting here—every ghoulish detail playing in her mind, over and over and over again.

Her statement made little sense to him, but he figured any information at this point was a good starting place. He could always have them reiterate and clear up any confusions later, when they were less frazzled. "Okay, that's question number one, so let's try a second one. Why didn't you call the police? Dial *911*," Joe asked. He'd asked this earlier, but hoped he'd get more than a "we didn't know who else to call" this time around. Although he doubted the interview would get more coherent, since they both seemed to be deteriorating right before his eyes. He needed to get answers faster, before they required a visit upstairs to have the physician-on-call give them a Xanax prescription. "You know that by removing the bodies, you've contaminated the crime scene."

"We did call," Parker murmured, rubbing the back of his neck. He massaged his muscles, but the knots refused to loosen. So tense were they, he felt as if his neck would snap if he twisted it too far on his shoulders.

"Yes, you did," the sheriff said patiently, "but not until *after* you'd brought them here. Are you aware that by moving them, you've disturbed the scene of what could very well have been murder? That's what you implied, yeah?"

"No," Mandy and Parker whispered simultaneously.

"Nothing there," Mandy said.

"Nothing left," Parker added.

"Pardon?"

Parker looked up, his gaze distant again, as if he were back at the scene of the crime, "There's no way anything escaped that heat. No evidence. And if we hadn't gotten them out, there'd be nothing of them left either."

Joe shook his head slightly to try to dispel the confusion swirling about in his brain. That was twice they'd relayed something, seemingly coherent, but which made zero sense to him. It also didn't pass his notice that they'd used the word *heat* twice during their recounting. "There was a fire?" he asked, trying to penetrate the maze of confusion.

"No fire," Mandy murmured, her gaze as vacant as that of her fiancé.

"No fire? I'm not sure I'm following you two in the least," the sheriff grumbled, holding on to his patience by sheer willpower. "If there wasn't a fire, then how—"

"Heat," Parker repeated. "Like an oven. Only not an oven."

"We don't know how," Mandy interjected, intuitively answering the sheriff's unasked question. "We heard bumps, banging, noises. Terrible, terrible noises."

"When we reached the fifth floor," Parker picked up the story, "and opened the door from the stairwell. The heat...oh, God, the heat was unbearable! And the scream...oh God!"

"Just *heat*," the sheriff repeated, trying to mask the incredulous tone in his voice. "You didn't see flames? Didn't feel the need to call the fire department?"

"No fire," they both repeated.

"So, let me get this straight," the sheriff sighed, swiping a hand in exhaustion across his face, "what you're saying is that there was a heat so severe that it mangled three bodies into unidentifiable cadavers, but there were no flames coupled with that heat. Am I understanding you correctly?"

Parker and Mandy nodded.

"So, if the heat was so insufferable, how did you get to the bodies without getting burned yourselves?" The sheriff was certain he'd found the very flaw in their stories that he'd been searching for; a big enough flaw to give him just enough cause to keep them hole up in his jail cell for a bit. Give him more time to investigate their involvement without lawyers mucking everything up. Then they responded and his confusion mounted.

"Turned off," Parker muttered.

"The heat? You turned it off? How? And why did you wait until those three on the slab in there were cooked like on an outdoor grill?" The sheriff started trying to keep his annoyance at the two firmly in check, but when they finally answered his questions, he wanted to strangle them both.

"The ghosts turned the heat off," Parker replied.

The sheriff leaned back in his chair, drawing deep breaths through his nostrils, "Okay, we're going to backtrack, because I'm not following this at all, and, quite frankly, I'm having a difficult time with everything you two are telling me. Let's start with where this took place."

"Monterey Cliffs—"

"The rundown sanatorium on the hill," Joe clarified, his tone flat.

He closed his eyes to the memories that assaulted him at the mention of that place and pulled his mental cloak of professionalism about himself. "Okay, why were you two there?"

"I bought it and—" Mandy started, stumbling over the reason why she'd gone up there. She knew her reasons were sound, but telling someone else those reasons may not sound reasonable.

"And?" Joe persisted.

"I'd hired a company to…um…determine if the place was really haunted." Mandy knew she was brushing over the actual reason, but to her it wasn't pertinent. The only thing that mattered was that three people were dead and the ghosts of Monterey Cliffs were responsible.

"I see," Joe muttered, "Okay, now. We know that three people died there, and even though the *how* is seriously in question, we'll get back to that. Right now, let's discuss the *why* you moved them. I know what you told me, but what is causing me a great deal of anxiety is that you moved them so far away from where it happened. You both know that my anxiety stems from the contamination to my crime scene, although you are convinced that there isn't a crime scene, so we'll come back to that too. So, you moved them to prevent more damage to the bodies, correct? That's what you both agree was necessary?"

Mandy and Parker nodded.

"So, why not just move them out of the room into the corridor or even out into the courtyard…what?" He asked when Mandy and Parker sat shaking their heads. "Why not?"

"We didn't know if they'd be safe anywhere up there, or that we'd be," Mandy whispered. "We just knew we had to get out of there."

"Okay, plausible. So, why the morgue? Why not come straight to the police station?"

"We went to the emergency room," Mandy said softly. "I remember passing it en route to the property, and it was the only place I could think of to go, in case—" she stumbled and couldn't finish the thought, but Joe knew what she was going to say—in case one of the three just happened to still be alive.

"The orderlies brought the bodies here to the morgue," Parker added, "and thought it best that we come too, so that when you arrived, we'd be available—"

"Okay," Joe interrupted, "I've gotten a clearer picture now—for at least some of my questions. So now, let's get back to what you saw that would make you say that *heat* was responsible for the deaths."

TWENTY

Upon hearing their reiteration of what had happened, the sheriff needed more of a break from the questioning than his suspects did, so headed back into the autopsy room. Frank saw him enter and quickly covered one of the bodies he was examining.

"So, Joe, what did they say?" Frank moved to stand between Joe and the examining table.

"Ghosts," Joe muttered. He'd hoped that by asking again, they'd trip up somehow and provide a more plausible explanation, but they'd stuck to their belief that somehow ghosts had been the cause of the *heat* that had caused the deaths of the three on the slab.

"Ghosts? Are you sure you heard them correctly?"

"Yep. Asked them twice at two separate times." Joe cracked the tension from his neck repetitively. "Damn, I need a drink." He was fully aware of the rumors that circulated in town about the hauntings at the old sanatorium on the hill, but as an adult of reasonable persuasion, he took them for what they were—tourist-driven fairy tales. Never in his entire career however, had anyone dared try using that folk tale as a defense for murder. As a means of explaining inexplicable disappearances—like with the college students from a few years back—but never as an argument for murder.

"So, I thought you said you'd be out to come get me in a second. Tell me what you discovered. Instead, you leave me out there with loopy and loony."

The medical examiner grinned, "I stepped out, but you were so busy with the interrogation that I figured I'd serve a better purpose trying to find out what answers these bodies held, until I get a forensic examiner in here anyway; but now you're saying that this was caused by *ghosts*."

"Hell, no! That isn't what I'm saying, that's what *they're* saying, but it wouldn't matter if Sigourney Weaver said it, I still wouldn't buy it for all the tea in China. I am sick to death of people placing the blame for anything and everything on culprits of the transparent variety."

"Well, you said it. You know as well as I do that the town folk believe that the old place is—"

"Don't even say it! Damn it all, Frank! If news leaks out that supports those nutcases in the village, we'll have every freak show from as far away as Timbuktu trying to spot a ghost, test their courage, or come kill someone so they can blame the local poltergeists."

"So, what you're saying is that you want me, and the pathologist, to try to find out what happened to these three individuals without drawing attention to your investigation, and at the same time scrounge up evidence that contradicts those two young people's story out there. That about sum it up?"

"Give me a break, Frank, okay?"

"I wish I could, Joe, but early indications are that these bodies were roasted by an immense heat, and there's damage to the tracheas, which suggest that they were alive when the heat began to engulf them."

"Shit! Wentworth mentioned hearing a scream. Damn, those poor kids! But you used the same word as they did—heat. You mean a fire, don't you?"

"No, not a fire. Heat. That's one thing those two got right. There's a difference in trace, which made that easy to determine. The hard part is figuring out the heat *source*, which I'm hoping the forensic pathologist will be able to do when he gets here. I still wanted to see if I couldn't provide some answers to alleviate my own confusions, and though their bodies are melded into a molten mess, there is no scorching present to indicate that it was caused by a flame of any kind."

"Great! Just great! Could you at least give me some good news? Like a non-phantasmal method that could do the same thing?"

"Sure, but at this point it would be conjecture and it sure as shootin' wouldn't be anything you'd find in an antiquated building, or that could be broken down or easily hidden after disposing of a body…"

"You're going to say an oven, aren't you?"

"Of a sort, yeah," Frank replied, arching his brow, "but it would have to be an oven of alien origin—one colossal unit that operated with some massive *internal* heating elements. Something heated as in a retort yet didn't annihilate by fire. Think you'll find something like that at that old sanatorium, or do you think those kids out there got rid of it before they brought the bodies in here?"

"Not funny. You wouldn't happen to have been eavesdropping on our conversation out there, would you?" Joe asked, remembering the explanation about the vanishing heat source his two prime suspects, his only suspects, fed him not a half hour earlier. "Never mind. I'm sure you'll come up with a logical explanation that doesn't lead me to a suspect recently hailed from—"

"The underworld? You know, Joe, there are industrial-sized ovens that might could be responsible for this, but from what I *did* overhear when I stepped out, it doesn't hold with what those two were telling you. And even if that old sanatorium held an oven of that type…would it still be functioning decades later? Wouldn't hurt to find out, I suppose. That might make the investigation go a little smoother if that were the case."

"Yeah, well, since I'm not certain that I'm getting straight answers from those two right now, we'll just go with it being one of those industrial ovens…at least until my investigation turns up something else that it could be. In the meantime, I'll do my best, as always, to find answers, but this one has me stumped. Ghosts surely can't be the only viable answer."

"I hope not, since you can't arrest ghosts."

"Well, I'd better get them two down to the precinct and get their statements in writing before they forget what they said, or before they lawyer up. Then I guess I'd best see to notifying whatever next of kin those three may have had." Joe lowered and shook his head.

"It doesn't seem to get any easier with time, does it?" Frank said softly.

Joe ran a hand through his hair, "You know, I told the police shrink that each of these grey hairs is the result of someone's death. A reminder never to forget how ugly this job is, and yet every time I look in the mirror, I'm thankful I'm still alive to see each one of those grey hairs. God, those poor kids!"

"I'll call you as soon as we find something, Joe, but I wouldn't hold my breath for this to turn out the way you want."

"No case ever seems to. Just send over the results when you get them," Joe pushed through the swinging doors and sighed again. An attorney had arrived, and Joe couldn't help but wonder which of the two young people had made that call, and whether it was just habit to do so in a time of trouble. After what Frank had told him though, an attorney wasn't needed right now, since his just cause had vanished like a puff of smoke. He couldn't hold them as suspects as long as the medical examiner was inadvertently providing collaboration of their stories.

He walked over to where the two still sat and was immediately confronted by the attorney of Amanda Bartonelli, chest puffed out like a rooster, "I hope that you're going to allow these two young people to leave soon," he asserted forcefully.

"There's a lot that doesn't make sense about what they've told me, but there isn't any reason for me to hold them right now. Once they've had the opportunity to calm down and get over the shock of what's happened, I'd like them to come back to the station so that we can get their statements formally, and, of course, it would behoove them to stay in town until the investigation wraps up. I do need them to head up to the hospital ward to change out of their clothing. I'll need it for trace evidence since this is a murder investigation. I'm sure that you have no objection to that. And it probably would do them good to see a physician while they're up there, and maybe set up a time to speak with a psychologist. They've been through the ringer this evening. After that, would you mind seeing them safely to wherever it is they're staying?"

The attorney nodded, deflating when he realized he wasn't going to have to do battle with the local law at all.

"Oh, and one more thing," Joe stated, "when Miss Bartonelli is less disconcerted, ask her to provide the information on those three in the morgue, so that I can see about getting in touch with next of kin."

The attorney nodded again, and Joe headed for the exit. With his two witnesses on the verge of collapse, his only avenue opened until they calmed enough to question again, was to go up to the sanatorium and have a look-see for himself. Hopefully find an oven. And if there were ghosts up at the old place, it was time he made their acquaintance.

TWENTY-ONE

Joe leaned against his Jeep Wrangler and stared up at the aged, decrepit, eclectic building that had been the center of many a controversy and could appreciate why it conjured so many imaginings; why it became the epicenter of so many disappearance investigations. People had an irrational need to believe in the paranormal, and this monstrosity gave them a place to house those ghostly beings.

An interview with a distraught parent had brought him here the first time to this legendary house of horrors, in the spring of ninety-three. He mentally replayed the interview with Kathleena Chauncey, the mother of Stephen Chauncey, one of three college students who had purportedly taken a hike up this ridge in April of that year.

"What made you think they were headed up to the old sanatorium, Mrs. Chauncey?" He'd asked during his initial interview after the missing person's report reached his desk. Joe knew it was a dim-witted question because he knew what the answer would be; however, his training and years of service had taught him to never overlook, or fail to ask, the obvious because sometimes the obvious turned into the unexpected. Such was the case during this interview.

"Stephen told me that they were going to try to capture some footage to substantiate the town folks' claims that the old place is haunted." Her voice trembled, on the verge of tears.

There was the obvious response Joe expected, but it was her next statement that validated his reason for always asking his perceived inane question:

"Go talk to Joey Trist—if he'll talk to you. He was with Stephen and another friend of theirs from college—Kevin, I believe his name was."

There was the unexpected. The missing person's report had been in error. It stated that *three* college-aged boys had gone missing during a hike up the mountain, but Mrs. Chauncey was saying that only two were missing and that one was anything but gone. Why hadn't he been informed of this immediately, and how had the boy been taken somewhere without someone notifying him? He didn't know; all he did know was that he needed to talk to Joey if he had any hopes of closing the case.

"Where can I find Joey, Mrs. Chauncey?"

"Saint Peter's Memorial Hospital. Psyche ward."

The sheriff stood, leaning against his Jeep, recollecting that first interview, still stumped over how Joey Trist could have been spirited away to a psyche ward without his finding out. He'd begun his investigation under the presumption that all three men had gone missing.

Even more disturbing was *why* everyone kept quiet about it, even when he'd discovered the truth and they knew he'd discovered the truth. Their silence angered him. No one interviewed during the course of that investigation had an answer to his queries, and Joe was certain he knew why no one had answers. The rich protect their own, and someone felt as if Joey needed protection from something that had taken place up here during the spring of nineteen ninety-three. He went in search of Joey and, as told, found him at the Saint Peter's Memorial Hospital psyche ward.

The silence of the townspeople confused Joe, but his interview with Joey left him completely mystified. He shook his head as he recalled Joey's events from that spring, de ja vu gripping him, because Joey's accounts were not far removed from the accounts of the two he'd just interviewed at the morgue. Yet Joe still refused to believe.

TWENTY-TWO

April 1993

"Where should we start searching first?" Joey asked as they all stood in the foyer, shivering partly from the pre-spring temperatures and partly from fear.

"Dude, this place is seriously spine-chilling," Kevin whispered, "and there are so many floors and rooms that we could search for a decade and not find a ghost. Unless every nook and cranny is haunted."

"Kevin's right, Stephen. What if there is only one spot that's haunted? We'll never find it before we have to head back down the mountain. It may not take a decade, but it could take hours; and we don't want to be in here for hours. We certainly aren't spending the night here. Not anymore."

"We'll split up—" Stephen started but was cut off in mid-thought.

"Ah, hell no!" Kevin and Joey said in concert.

"If this place is phantom ridden, we'll be in a world of hurt if we split up," Joey retorted and his face flushed at the look sent his way by Stephen. "What?" He snapped.

"Your logic is flawed, and you're allowing fear to dictate your actions," Stephen replied haughtily. "It won't matter if we stay together or if we split up. We wouldn't stand a chance against ghosts either way; or do you think if we combine our brawn and brains it is going to scare away the baddies? Logically, we each have a video camera and can cover more ground before we leave here later today. If even one of us manages to capture footage, then it will have been worth a little terror, don't ya think? Staying together limits the chances of us locating anything and does nothing for safety. Come on, Kevin; back me up here, man! You know I'm right."

"We should each take designated floors and meet back up front by three p.m.," Kevin murmured, a little reluctantly. "We'll need to be

127

headed back to town no later than that. Agreed?"

"So, you in, Joey?" Stephen asked.

Joey's heart was racing, but Stephen was right. Other than a beer can to the head, a corpse sliding down a chute, and a stunning specter with slit wrists, he had no reason but rumor to spur his fears. If he could tamp that down, he could walk through his designated floor, record some footage, and be out the door before a ghost decided he was a nuisance that needed to be dealt with. He nodded his consent.

"Awesome! So, after looking at the plans," Stephen exclaimed enthusiastically, "the floors, most likely to be ripe with hauntings, are the fifth floor, the fourth floor, and the sixth floor. If we still have time after exploring those, we'll meet up to do a quick tour of the other floors. Sound cool?"

"You make it sound like a Disneyland adventure," Joey muttered. When Stephen shot a disgruntled gaze in his direction he quickly added, "I'll take the sixth floor." Later, he would realize that his choice would save his life.

TWENTY-THREE

Stephen climbed the steps down from the sixth floor to the fourth floor, still scratching his head mentally as to why the elevator didn't stop at the fourth or fifth floors, even though they'd punched the *4* and *5*.

"The ghosts probably don't want people visiting those particular floors," Kevin had joked.

"That doesn't make sense, because people can simply get there via the stairwell," Joey countered.

"Unless we get up to those doorways and they end up being welded shut by some spectral forces."

When they'd realized that the elevator was malfunctioning, and they stepped out into the sixth-floor corridor, any humor Stephen felt fled inexplicably, replaced by a vice-like fear that gripped his heart so tightly that he found it difficult to breathe. Without knowing why, he suddenly wanted to take Joey's advice about the buddy system. Stay together. But it had been his idea to split up to begin with and he certainly didn't want his friends to perceive him as a wuss, so he drew in deep silent breaths so as not to give away the anxiety that was suffusing his entire body, until finally he began to calm.

"Okay, Joey, we'll leave you to explore this floor," Kevin said, heading toward the stairwell. "Come on, Stephen. Let's go."

Stephen could do no more than nod and follow. When they reached the fifth-floor landing, both men looked at each other—one wondering whether the door would open, the other hoping it wouldn't. It did.

Kevin moved from the landing into the fifth-floor corridor wearing a smirk that belied his own nervousness, "See you in a bit," he said as the door closed slowly behind him.

Stephen remained rooted for several minutes, shining the light of his flashlight all around him, forcing his breathing to remain steady.

He closed his eyes for a second, bolstering his courage, then started down to his designated floor.

He continued his attempted mental bolstering as he descended the paltry twenty-step distance from the fifth to fourth floor, allowing the beam from his flashlight to guide his way. He reached the fourth floor and wavered apprehensively for a fraction of a second, hoping as he had a few moments earlier, that the door wouldn't open. He lifted his hand slowly and placed it on the latch and drew in a deep breath, holding it as he pushed the lever down. He closed his eyes when he heard it click and sighed in disappointment when it opened.

All his bravado earlier when they'd arrived, and his attempts to boost his courage during his trek from the sixth floor, vanished again as his heart began pulsating deafeningly in his ears, and his palms began sweating enough to fill a milk jug. He swiped them on his pants leg and aimed his flashlight beam down each length of the hallway. It didn't shine far and so afforded little comfort.

While he was resolute in his determination to capture footage of a ghost, he was also petrified over encountering one. Feeling as he did now made him question his assertion that each of them should explore individually. His logic as to why had been sound, but the overwhelming fear enveloping him now made him wish he had someone by his side.

"You and your stupid ideas," he muttered, sucking in deep breaths through his nostrils. "Stupid or not, you're going to have to do something because you'll look like a real dick if they capture something on film and you come back with nothing but a pants full of shit."

That thought worked to shake loose the worst of his fears and he began to breathe a little easier again. When he reminded himself of why he chose this particular floor to explore, his breathing calmed to normal.

He knew he should feel bad over selecting this floor without giving his friends the benefits of his reasoning, but Joey had jumped at the chance to commune with the spirit of children, and Kevin didn't seem to mind being relegated to the fifth floor, so he wasn't going to allow guilt to eat at him too much.

Besides, it wasn't as if he was one-hundred percent certain that his reasons were great ones. Still, he was fairly confident that any ghosts that inhabited the fourth floor would be of the innocuous variety.

Falling back on logic, as he always did, his conclusion stemmed from his research. This floor may have appeared the more malevolent within the facility, as many an unauthorized surgery or shock therapy purportedly occurred within one of the fourth-floor rooms; however, as those patients who had endured atrocity were most likely haunting the reefs at the bottom of the ocean, that left only ghosts in white lab coats who harbored feelings of guilt for performing illicit experiments on the many hapless patients that resided here. Harmless physicians—or at least harmless in death.

He also failed to share his enthusiasm over getting choice of this floor, since logic also dictated that he'd be able to escape faster if he did encounter a specter with an attitude. Being closer to the exit had its advantages; or so he presumed.

TWENTY-FOUR

Kevin, just like Stephen, simply stood rooted just inside the doorway, allowing his light to light up the walls, floor, and ceiling, while he worked hard to talk himself into actually exploring. He may have come off as glib when he parted company with his friends, but he felt anything but that way in his gut and spent considerable time trying to bolster his own courage.

After a few minutes of telling himself he had nothing to be afraid of, he lifted his video camera, hit record, and started down the corridor. He decided to turn it on now because it had a built-in flashlight, which was more powerful than his hand-held flashlight; and because he'd already missed two extraordinary ghost-recording opportunities, so was determined to be at the ready this time.

He recalled some interesting tidbits about this floor that Stephen revealed. The mundane facts though were that this floor was thought to be the housing wing for patients, both in the twenties, when it was a mental facility, and again in the sixties, when it was an institute for the elderly. The interesting tidbits surrounded an association to the small town at the base of the mountain. Two of the residents, during both of those eras, had the same surname as one who'd frequented the small town over the years—Bartonelli.

Amanda Bartonelli may not have lived in the town, but she had attended college with one of the residents, Anne Chauncey—Joey's older sister—and would often spend holidays and summer vacations with the Chauncey family. When Stephen brought up the Bartonelli name during their chats about the facility while at college, Kevin could hear the affection in Stephen's tone. One day, Joey revealed that he and Stephen would often fanaticize of marrying Amanda Bartonelli, even though she was years older.

Stephen also revealed one evening during their chats at college, that when he was younger, he'd overheard Mandy talking to Anne about one ghost in particular—Mandy's grand aunt Maria. That story, Kevin was certain, is what spurred Stephen into making this trek for proof over a decade later—more so than money or fame. Despite his protestations, Kevin didn't doubt that Stephen wanted to capture Mandy's grand aunt Maria on video, so that he could impress Mandy. There was such a fond tone when reminiscing over Amanda Bartonelli that it surprised Kevin when Stephen chose to explore the fourth floor, instead of this one. Not that it mattered to Kevin, since proof was proof, no matter who happened to capture that proof, and he wasn't going to complain since he knew this floor would likely house ghosts of the safe variety. He was convinced that old folks wouldn't harm a soul in life—or in death. He felt fortunate he'd gotten this floor to explore.

Kevin kept his camera aimed ahead as he trekked to room *502*, a room of infamy in town equal to the sanatorium. It was here that the Bartonelli women resided during their stay at this establishment— which everyone always bandied about as highly coincidental; however, the other occurrence, which made the room notorious, was that a young nurse ostensibly hung herself from the rafters, ending not only her own life but that of her unborn child.

If there is a room housing ghosts here, it'll be this one, Kevin thought, stopping before the very room of his musings.

TWENTY-FIVE

Joey wanted to climb back into the elevator, after Stephen and Kevin left down the stairwell, but he knew that neither of his friends would let him live it down if he missed the opportunity of filming a ghostly encounter. At least he'd chosen the floor of the children's ward. Rumor had it that one particular child by the name of Jimmy, was a friendly sort that loved to cavort with visitors. That was one haunting he could deal with. What he couldn't stomach was the thought of running into a poltergeist with an attitude, like the one who'd hit him with the beer can, although none were rumored to inhabit the rooms of this establishment. Still, he would rather not take that chance. Before he could change his mind and actually hang out in the elevator car for the next hour or two, he quickly made his way to the room that Jimmy was supposed to inhabit.

He'd stood inside the door for no more than a minute when a ball rolled in his direction. He quickly removed his video camera and set it in the corner of the room. He punched record, and then turned to look at where the ball had rolled again and come to rest near his feet.

"Is that Jimmy playing with the ball?" The ball rolled away a bit, and then back in his direction. He lightly kicked it across the room and was astonished when it stopped suddenly beneath the window, as if contacting an invisible wall.

"Wow!" Joey murmured. "Nice intercept, Jimmy. I hope the others are meeting ghosts are pleasant as you. Think that's possible?" Joey wasn't surprised that his query went unanswered, but he did hold onto the hope that his friends' encounters—if any—would be equally innocuous.

TWENTY-SIX

Stephen turned to his left and traversed part way down the passageway of the fourth floor before drawing another conclusion; this one more unsteadying than the last. None of the rooms were numbered or marked in any way. There was nothing along the corridor that stood out, nothing that announced the purpose of each of these rooms. The first-floor rooms had been clearly marked—infirmary, solarium, kitchen, dining facility—but on this floor, there was nothing. It was eerily uninviting in its sameness.

If not for the chute originating from the window, patently announcing use of this floor, one may suspect it to have been vacant during its time of tenancy. Glancing at each of the doors, Stephen began to rethink why these rooms were unmarked. Could it be that the occupants of this floor preferred anonymity for their work? Perhaps they didn't wish for anyone, coming up here, to know what each room was designated for. There was also a rumor that circulated, along with all the other rumors, that in the twenties, the elevator didn't even stop at the fourth floor; that the only access was by stairwell and only certain people had a key to unlock the door leading to this floor. His brow knitted. The elevator had been replaced in the sixties, but even though he'd punched the button for the fourth floor—and the fifth—the elevator had moved right past them, on to the sixth. Did that mean anything? Did it not stopping at the fourth floor in the twenties mean anything? It certainly meant nothing to him—other than providing another reason for him to feel creeped out as he crept along the corridor staring at non-descript doorways.

He reached the end of the corridor and turned; staring down the length of the hallway as far as his light permitted, and then he made his third observation. He had not encountered a single entity during that short stroll, which meant that either this floor wasn't haunted, or he was going to have to venture into the rooms to detect that which he sought. He shuddered, and then started back down the corridor.

This time however, he opened each door as he went, reluctantly peering into the darkness; yet too fearful to venture inside.

He wasn't certain what he anticipated discovering in each room, but a dark void full of nothingness certainly hadn't been on his list of expectations. As the doors were minus any designated markings, so too the rooms demonstrated futility in identifying which was used for what purpose. As he opened more doors, revealing more emptiness, he began to think the chute, yet another engineering faux pas and this floor was indeed nothing more than a fallow adjunct. He reached the stairwell with nothing to show for his short stint on the fourth floor than raw nerves and an irritated psyche.

"Time to make a decision, Stephen," he murmured, "head back down to wait for your friends, go meet up with one of them; or stick with it and check out the other rooms. May just be that one of them will reveal the location of the chute and hold more content than a dark empty space." He glanced at his watch. He still had an hour of exploration left before the given deadline. If the rest of the rooms were as unrewarding as the other rooms, he could easily check out the remaining ten or so with time to spare.

With a sigh, he stepped across the hall and opened the next door, ready to explore as many as were necessary to find what he sought.

TWENTY-SEVEN

"Bingo!" Stephen declared triumphantly, after nearing the opposite end of the hallway.

The minute his light penetrated the darkness, Stephen knew that he'd located the room of legend. That room in which many a campfire ghost story originated; in which wretched patients became involuntary victims of the medical profession. This room was not barren as the others had been it held tables and tools—antiquated surgeon's tools—all coated in a film of grime, as if untouched for decades.

Stephen took a step inside, tentatively casting his light from corner to corner, as if to ward off any unhappy demons lurking about in the shadows. He aimed his light at the floor and quivered at the stark contrast in hues—gray and rust—floor and blood. It never registered that the equipment furnishing this room was out of place—out of sync with the era during which this facility was used to house geriatric patients. The tables and tools would only have been found here during the twenties and early thirties from whence came the stories of the macabre. It didn't dawn in his mind that these things would have been removed when ownership was transferred in the sixties—unless the doctor had kept them out of his own ghoulish fascination with the experimentations in the earlier decades. But for Stephen, sense at finding these things still here decade upon decade later, didn't register in his logical mind as out of place—out of time. He was just too pleased that he'd found something.

"Well, here's my chance," he murmured. He slid the flashlight beneath his pants belt, and then pulled his video camera from his shoulder. He flicked the *on* switch, followed by the video lamp, and then pressed *record.* He lifted the viewfinder to his eye and whispered, "Here, ghosty, ghosty. Time to make Stephen a millionaire!"

The door slammed violently, powerfully, shaking the floor beneath Stephen's feet. He jumped and let out a squeal that would have embarrassed his baby sister. Body quaking, he jerked his camera in the direction of the door. He let out another startled squeal as the light connected momentarily with his phantom menace, but his fear was not so concentrated as to overlook the negative reaction the light had on the ghost. The specter winced at the sudden glare in its eyes and lurched aside. Stephen held fast to the video camera with a will aided only by survival instincts and moved the light on the bearing in which the phantasm had staggered. He spun slowly, arching the light in all directions, determined to keep the ghost unhinged and to regain his own poise.

After a complete revolution, he sighed in simultaneous disappointment and relief, and then stepped slowly back toward the door. He had his tale to tell, and hopefully footage to back it up. He'd seen what he saw, and, by God, he didn't ever want to see it again. It was time to go. If his friends got even close to what he got, they'd be millionaires for certain.

He turned to open the door and let out a blood-curdling scream.

TWENTY-EIGHT

Joey heard a loud, heart-piercing scream emit from below his floor, but as with the ball that continually returned, as if playing fetch with an invisible dog, he wasn't certain if it were illusory or genuine. He closed his eyes in fear and indecision, wanting to assist, but more than that, wanting to live. He wrapped his arms around his shivering body, but the quakes wouldn't abate. He opened his eyes and gasped. Standing beside him, staring in horror at the door to the room, was a little boy. Jimmy, he presumed.

Whatever it was that he'd heard hadn't been an illusion because the boy appeared to have heard it also, and it scared him into showing himself, but when the little ghost turned it look up at him, it wasn't fear he saw in his gaze, but questioning.

"I can't," Joey declared, assuming that the question was 'why don't you go see what's happening?'. The boy's brow furrowed in disapproval, confirming those very expectations.

He then lifted his finger and pointed toward the door, but Joey just stood rooted, staring down into young eyes filled with condemnation, "There wouldn't be screaming if everything was okay," Joey tried to reason. "What do you think I could accomplish against whatever it is that's causing the screams?"

The little boy stood there, continuing to stare at him unblinking, then whispered one word, "Go!"

Joey didn't need further prompting. The boy may have wanted him to go check on his friend, but Joey was just going to get out. He dashed into the corridor and ran for the stairwell, pulling open the door with such force, one of the hinges—rusted with time—pulled away from the wall. Without slowing, he took the stairs two at a time, slipping, and falling repeatedly in his haste to leave. He fell as he leapt down the steps, bumping his head against the wall. He lie there stunned, but another blood-curdling cry rent the air, and he realized it was coming from the corridor outside which he now lie.

He stood slowly, his knees knocking audibly, tears streaming down his cheeks. He hadn't run as far as he'd thought, because before him on the wall was a big number *4*. The floor that Stephen said that he was going to explore. Joey stood in indecision. It was all quiet now, making him wonder whether what he'd heard had been real after all. Still, he was here now, all was quiet, and he could potentially assist whomever it was in trouble—if anyone was. He sucked in a deep breath of courage and reached for the doorknob.

His hand wrapped around the steel knob, then he yanked it back with a loud yelp. It was blazing hot. He stared at it, aghast. *What am I going to do?* He retreated away from the door until his back bumped into the wall, and then he slid down it, sitting with his knees drawn to his chest. *What am I supposed to do now?*

A thought jumped into his head, and he glanced quizzically upwards, suddenly realizing that Kevin hadn't come running to check on Stephen. Surely, he'd heard the screams since he was only one flight up. Joey's brain interpreted his absence to mean that Kevin had already fled, leaving him and Stephen to fend for themselves.

He cradled his hand, which still stung from touching the fire-hot doorknob, and shook his head in indecision, "What do I do? What do I do?"

Another yell of pain and terror rent the air, followed by a loud bang, and then silence; more terrifying than the screams had been. Joey was quaking violently, tears streaming down his cheek. It was obvious to him now that Stephen was in serious trouble and the only person within reach to help him was himself.

He stood, and nearly toppled over because the wobbling in his legs was so strong. He stepped toward the door, using the wall for support, then pulled his sleeve over his hand. He reached for the doorknob again, ready to suffer the pain in order to open it quickly. He braced himself, placed his hand on the knob and jerked back, not from pain but surprise. It felt cool; cold. He reached for it again and opened the door. With mounting fear, he stepped into the corridor, but without any idea of where to search for Stephen, he felt hopelessness overwhelm him.

"Stephen!" He yelled but received no response. He called out again and physically jumped when a man in a white frock coat appeared out of nowhere and started his way, his countenance menacing.

Joey cried out in terror and leapt back into the stairwell, jumping down the remaining steps. He slid across the foyer, nearly colliding with the front door in his haste to escape. He pushed it open and ran into the courtyard, skidding to a halt; thankful to be outside in the crisp evening spring air. He bent, placing his hands on his knees, drawing in deep, cleansing breaths. When he opened his eyes, he realized his breath was discernible and the temperature was falling. He stood and turned to look back at the building, his gaze inexplicably drawn toward the chute. He stared in muted terror as the body of his friend went hurtling into the water below.

He didn't need clinical detachment to know it had to be one of his friends—most likely Stephen—since the chute originated from the floor that Stephen had been, nor did it take an effort to realize that the body wasn't moving. No arms flailing, no feet kicking, no screaming. That left little doubt in Joey's mind that his friend had become a victim of the ghosts of Monterey Cliffs Sanatorium.

No further prompting was required. Forgetting that Kevin could possibly still be inside somewhere and potentially facing equal danger, Joey bolted, covering the distance from the courtyard to the town square in record time. He stopped in the center of Main Street, and then with a dramatic wail of anguish, collapsed.

* * * * * * * * *

The little boy on the sixth floor stood next the window, a deep sadness in his gaze as he watched the man who'd played ball with him dash away in fear. The sadness turned to anger as he thought of all of those who'd come before, willing to keep him company, only to be snatched away by those on the floors below. That anger welled inside his chest until he was fairly glowing with rage. His gaze spotted the camera in the corner, still recording. He glided over slowly, then started breathing heavily on the piece of equipment until the heat in his body dispelled and the camera turned to ash.

TWENTY-NINE

Kevin ceased the barrage of conventional questions one was purported to ask ghosts—not that he'd actually seen or heard one as yet. He turned off his tape recorder and cocked his head, listening. He'd heard screams, or had he? The sound had been faint, and too short-lived to be certain. He set his recorder down, stood up from where he'd been sitting the last half hour, and stepped to the door of room *502*, his head cocking from side to side, straining to hear anything, but he heard nothing but a faint bounding noise, as if someone was barreling down the stairs at breakneck speed, but even that ceased before he could ascertain its validity. He tapped on the door—solid oak. Definitely difficult for sound to penetrate, or for him to mishear anything that did. He pulled the door open, peering into the corridor. He heard not even a peep, so dismissed the noises as no more than auditory illusions—ceiling creaking, rats running through the walls…that last thought caused a shiver to race along his spine, and he flashed the beam of his light around the room to ensure there weren't any holes in the walls by which a rat could slip out and bite him. He'd be the one screaming then, if that happened.

When he felt less jittery over potential rat assault, he retrieved his recorder, sat back down in the center of the room, and resumed his standardized questioning session, "If there is anyone here, could you let me know how you died? Was it natural causes?"

Another faint noise penetrated the oak door, and he stood more swiftly, dashing over to open it. He moved back into the corridor to see if he could hear it better. This time, there was no mistaking it—a petrified scream reached his hearing, and he instinctually took a step back into the room and shut the door—as if that very door that prevented sound penetrating would protect him from whatever it was that was causing the screams. The hairs on the back of his neck and along his arms stood, and the cliché shiver raced along his spine. There was no chalking it up to auditory illusion that time. Someone in this place was screaming bloody murder. The only thing he wondered was whether it was friend or phantom.

He shook off the fear that immobilized him momentarily and headed back toward the door, determined to put bravery before terror; but this time it wouldn't open. He yanked and tugged at the knob, but it remained firmly shut. He lifted a hand to bang, but an unseen force grabbed his arm and yanked him backwards off his feet. He landed with a thud on his rear, his recorder crashing to the floor. He sat, stunned. His tailbone ached; his mind unable to register what had happened. The entire time he'd been in the room, he hadn't so much as heard a sound or seen an entity, but when he tried to leave, to go investigate screaming from another floor, something was determined to prevent it. But why? Was the ghost protecting him from something or was this entity in league with those causing the screams? He shook the thought from his mind, scared to dwell on what might lie in store for him if the poltergeist that pulled him to the floor was only getting started—and it was.

He had no chance to register what happened before the unidentifiable entity grasped hold of his feet and propelled his body towards the far wall. He slammed into the peeling green paint face first and felt his nose snap. He crumbled into a heap, but remained there only a fraction of a second before he was airborne again, his back slamming into another wall. He grunted and collapsed into another mass; his battered body aching, his vision dazed, and blood oozing into his open mouth and damaged sinuses. When no further attacks seemed forthcoming, he slid onto his belly and began inching his way toward the door, wincing in pain with each movement.

He scooted painfully to his knees and reached for the doorknob, silently willing it to turn. It did. He gripped the knob with both hands, pulling himself upright, and tugged the big oak door open. He sensed freedom, as he took one step into the corridor, but then two pair of hands grabbed hold of his ankles and yanked him off his feet. He fell face first. His nose would've penetrated his brain if he hadn't instinctually thrown his hands down to ease the blow, but it didn't stop his already damaged wrists snapping upon impact. He let out a piercing wail of agony that turned to whimpers of pain and horror as his gaze sought and found the beings dragging him down the corridor towards the stairwell.

His eyes widened at the distinct figures of two men in grey uniforms dragging him along as if he were a side of beef being hauled to the slaughterhouse. That last thought snapped him from his shock, and he tried to struggle, but his muscles were too bruised, too many bones broken. He set his mind to work on the task of freeing himself, since it was the only part of his body not currently damaged, but it too seemed unable to determine a way out of his current plight.

With no regard to his already pounded state, the ghostly forces hauled his body down the single flight of stairs, pitiless to his constant cries of pain as he was jolted violently the twenty steps to the next landing. When they lugged his body into the fourth-floor corridor, he was nearly unconscious. They slid his body along the tattered and moldy carpeting, then dumped him against a massive hole in the wall, and then they were gone. At least it seemed as if they were—no pulling, no tugging, no hurling against nearby structures. They just disappeared. It appeared he'd been deserted. He moaned as he struggled to right himself, so he could self-assess. He wasn't certain about all the damage he'd suffered, but breathing was difficult, so he knew he had some broken ribs to go along with his broken nose; he couldn't raise his arm, so he determined he had a dislocated shoulder, and when he tried to stand, his leg gave out from beneath him with a shooting pain through his entire groin area, which told him his hip was likely disjointed or broken. Either way, he knew he wasn't going to be leaving here on his feet. He slid back down against the wall and closed his eyes, preparing himself mentally to face the monumental task before him—getting himself free of this place before another ghost decided to finish him off.

He heard a noise behind him and turned his head to peer in the hole in the wall. The sight that met his gaze threatened to send him mentally crashing into an abyss.

Several men in white lab coats were attending to ill-looking, less-than-ecstatic patients. One patient was strapped to a chair, screeching hoarsely, as a doctor rammed a needle into his forehead—then he fell silent. Another doctor was focused on a table. He couldn't see the patient, but he could hear the screams and see the flailing limbs.

He shook the shock from his brain and turned away. How he was going to get out of his current predicament, he didn't know, but he knew he had to try before another poltergeist returned to drag him into that room to finish him off.

He stretched out into a prone position, stifling the screams that threatened to escape with each movement he made, but he knew that silence was his ally right now. He couldn't risk drawing the attention of those in that room. He reached out with his good arm, pulling himself, using his only good leg to assist in propelling forward. The pain jolting through his body was red hot, and his brain kept threatening to shut down; but he forced himself to push past the agony and keep moving; however, thoughts of getting down four flights of stairs, across a massive lobby, and down a mountainside, jarred him motionless again. He knew he'd never manage it. He sucked in air through his mouth and lie still, trying to decide what he was going to do; how he was going to survive this. The stairs alone would be more than he could bear. Then his mind supplied part of the answer—the elevator. He could use that to at least make getting free of the building more likely.

His neck ached when he turned his head to locate the dull shine of the elevator nearby, examining the potential of raising up sufficient distance to press the down button, then dragging his body into the car before the doors slid shut again. The idea of having those heavy doors pressing against his already tattered body had him looking toward the stairwell again. Bouncing along a flight of stairs, suddenly seemed preferable to being pounded and smashed by elevator doors.

He laid his head down for a moment to rest then began the slow excruciating pull along the old, dingy carpet. He'd just have to move as fast as he could, fight the pain—if he wanted to survive. His breathing was coming in distressed gasps by the time he reached the elevator doors. He'd arrived at his goal, but now was so fatigued, so drained of energy, in so much agony, that the push button seemed suddenly out of reach.

A fleeting thought brought a tear to his eye that he was going to die in this insane asylum after all, but he slammed the mental door shut on any negativity, "Think only of this first hurdle," he whispered encouragement to himself. "Worry about the next hurdle when you get to it. I don't care if it takes a week to get down this mountain, you're going to do it; because you don't want to become some poltergeist's next test subject."

With a deep intake of air to strengthen his resolve, he reached for the button. His finger pushed the cool surface, lighting the down arrow—and then a searing heat tore through his body, turning him to a pile of ashes through an all-consuming heat; his screams joining those of the ghostly patients at the Monterey Cliffs Sanatorium.

THIRTY

The sheriff continued leaning against his Jeep Wrangler, staring up at the old building as his mind lingered on Joey's accounting of events; but for the life of him, he could not wrap his brain around Joey's delusional recollection of what occurred. He sounded sane, yet completely insane simultaneously.

In nineteen ninety-three, Joe had made a trip up here when the three young men went missing, but he'd found nothing unusual, nothing out of place; and nothing that assisted in his investigation. Everything was locked up tight, the three immense chains and locks still attached to the equally massive front door, even though Joey claimed that Kevin had managed to pick all three open, which is how they'd gained entry. Yet, upon arrival, all three locks were secure, which meant that Joey had lied; that if the young men had gotten in, they'd climbed the structure and shimmied through a broken window somewhere. And if he'd lied about that, he could've lied about other things, including any, and all, elements of his story surrounding his friends' disappearances. To what end, he didn't know; and if it *were* all fanaticized, what had driven him to the brink of madness, landing him in the psyche ward for the past seven years. Something had traumatized him, caused him to create a story about his friends' disappearances, apparently a story far less devastating in his mind than the truth. But what could be more devastating than being assaulted and killed by ghosts?

The sheriff sighed heavily because he'd never found out. Joey Trist stopped talking, and no bodies were ever found. Because of the lack of evidence, the file on Stephen Chauncey and Kevin Banger remained in a file in his unsolved cases cabinet—a lone, thin file in a vast, otherwise empty, drawer.

Now, here he stood again, seven years after that event, staring up at the old building, with yet another inexplicable case to solve; and although the two surviving members were more than willing to talk, what they had to say sounded just as deluded as his interview with Joey Trist.

Ghosts they'd said by way of explanation. *Ghosts* had been Joey's explanation too. He'd dismissed both stories outright, but now, as his gaze moved slowly over the crumbing facade of the building, he began questioning whether ghosts were truly to blame for the devastation that tested the mental well-being of the surviving visitors to this establishment.

"I guess the only way to find out is to get inside and see for myself." He fumbled with the set of keys he'd taken from a reluctant Amanda Bartonelli. He grinned thinly as he recalled the look of horror in her eyes when he requested, she lend him her keys to the old place.

"I need to look around," he said as she started shaking her head, *"to ascertain for myself the validity of your statements."* She sat shaking her head, clutching her purse to her chest, and refusing to part with the keys.

"No! I won't be responsible for the deaths of any more people. I locked that place up tight, and I plan to call a demolition team on Monday and have the damnable place destroyed, and every demon along with it."

"I can't let you do that, Miss Bartonelli, not until I close my investigation. There may be evidence——"

"There is *no evidence!"* Mandy's vehement tone startled the sheriff, but he refused to relent. He wasn't simply going to take her word in an open homicide investigation.

"Mandy, listen to me. There were three men who came up here seven years ago, and two of those men went missing," the sheriff stated.

"I know about the men. One was the brother of a friend of mine," Mandy interjected softly.

"Then you know that those disappearances are also purportedly linked to that facility. If I am going to get answers as to why people keep going into that place

and not coming out, and why everyone who goes in there is certain that ghosts are at the heart of those disappearances; then I'm going to need to get in there to check it out. I can't just take your word that the current deaths are associated with poltergeists with bad attitudes. He saw the flicker of a grin flit across Mandy's lips, but it held no humor. Quickly it transformed into a quivering sob. She nodded, pulled open her purse, and extracted a ring of keys from the massive interior.

"If you die—" Mandy's words caught on a sob, and she couldn't continue. Her gaze implored the sheriff to reconsider his decision, but Joe ignored her visual plea and took the ring of keys from her hand, shaking in fear.

"If I die, I'll have deserved it. All I need to do is find proof that ghosts inhabit the place, preferably before kicking the bucket. If they do, I'll dial that demolition company for you on Monday. That should prevent further deaths and disappearances, yeah?"

As Joe fumbled with the keys, attempting to locate the three which corresponded to the locks, he began to question the wisdom of his decision. *If* those he'd interviewed were truly convinced of what they'd seen, he could very well be inviting his own demise. He could simply accept their word as fact and walk away, but it wasn't like him to accept other people's word; he needed to find proof for himself. He stopped for a moment and thought about radioing in for backup—just in case, but what was he going to tell his deputy? That he was afraid of a building because people were convinced it was haunted? He shook his head and returned to work on the locks.

"Still, it's not exactly your smartest move, Joe," he muttered as the first lock fell away from its colossal chain and clattered to the ground. The chain fell away next, pooling in a heap atop the lock. Joe went in search of the second key, sighing when the lock and chain joined the first on the ground. "One more to go," he mumbled, flipping the keys on the ring, trying each one.

The third lock and chain fell away, and Joe took a deep breath before pushing open the massive door. He stepped inside and waited a moment while his eyes adjusted to the shadowy inside, light from broken panes the only source chasing away the darkness.

He quickly oriented himself and wasted no time heading for the elevator. As he waited, listening to the creaks and moans associated with disuse as it squealed toward the lobby, his nerves started to leap. "I think that it might be better to climb the stairs. I don't like the sounds of that thing."

As he climbed, his mind recalled what every witness had recounted to him, which told him that the fourth or fifth floor was where he was likely to find the bogeymen who appeared to enjoy snuffing out life forms. He decided to start on the fifth floor because it was a room on that floor in which the three current victims were murdered. And since that room wasn't likely to house an oven, he was at a loss—again—as to explain the condition of those victims. Amanda Bartonelli and Parker Wentworth said that heat radiated in the corridor, which was why they couldn't reach the three ghost chasers. So then, what caused the heat; and what was he likely to encounter when he traversed that same corridor to the room of infamy.

When he reached the landing of the fifth floor, he stopped and leaned against the wall. Not because he needed the rest, but because he thought it a good time to send up a prayer.

"Okay, Lord, I'm here. I don't know if there are any ghosts here, and if there are, why they didn't leave this place once their bodies were no longer needed. You know I happen to be of the belief that our energy just kind of dissipates into space once it departs our bodies, so I'm not much of a believer in apparitions; however, I'm not dumb enough to rule out much of anything, especially when others, just as reputable as myself, appear convinced that ghosts exist and are causing harm. If that be the case, and you happen to know of these specters, would you be so inclined as to ask them to spare my life, so I can finally put to rest the number of cases mounting surrounding this decrepit old building? I'd be much obliged."

He placed a hand on the doorknob; reluctant to open it for fear that he would see a gargantuan oven, with cartoonish-sharpened snapping teeth, waiting and ready to consume him. He shook the anxiety from his mind and pushed the door wide. He was slightly disappointed to see nothing before him but a corridor, dimly lit from the rays of the sun shining from a window on the far end. He sighed, from both relief and disappointment, and took a step tentatively into the hallway. He held his breath, ready to jump back onto the landing, should a ghoul with a warped sense of humor decide to flick a switch and scorch his feet, as two of his current witnesses attested had happened, not precisely to them, but in their sight.

When nothing occurred, he sighed loudly. He could hear his heart pounding in his ears as he turned toward room *502*.

THIRTY-ONE

Sheriff Joe Montgomery stared at the numbers on the door, dull and rusty, a look of comical indecision etched on his face. He popped the kinks from his neck and gazed up and down the corridor, his breathing shallow and his heart racing. Here was the decisive moment. He had traversed the hallway without incident and had stood before this door more than five minutes without a phantom with a morbid sense of the macabre attempting to roast him alive. Now all he needed to do was enter the villainous room of death and attempt contact with one of its occupants; and then pray that said occupant didn't take a dislike to him or his presence. As before, he gripped the doorknob with trepidation, and with no hesitation, swung the door wide.

Nothing.

Absolutely nothing met his gaze, save for a conventionally furnished bedroom: antiquated and tattered, dusty, and grim. That was the first observation that Joe found oddly and eerily disturbing. He expected there to be something ethereal, in feeling if not in view. There was nothing. Yet, this room, specifically, had been one mentioned in the interviews, as being particularly of interest. Perhaps he'd heard wrong, or perhaps he'd gotten this mixed up with the other room of infamy: the autopsy room.

Was it this room or the autopsy room, in which his two distraught witnesses assured him had nothing remaining after the annihilation of the Specter Detectors? That the intense heat had reduced every piece of furniture to an unrecognizable molten mass.

But while these furnishings were aged and ruinous, they were identifiable; and while a film of dust covered everything remaining in the room, he could not see where anything had been reduced to rubble from a fire—or heat. Certainly nothing had been turned into an unidentifiable molten mass. He began to question everything he'd heard.

502. He was certain that's what he'd written, so either he'd misheard or what they'd seen was not real. He stepped back into the hall and checked the number again on the door: *502*. Had he heard incorrectly?

He moved back into the room and peered behind the door, not certain what he expected to find, hoping to discover something. When no one jumped at him from behind the door, he hesitantly moved further into the room and across the floor toward the window. Occasionally, he glanced down at the floor to make certain it didn't start glowing red around his feet. He grinned when he made it without dying.

He closed his eyes and tried to visualize the writing in his report, which he'd inconveniently left lying on the seat of his Jeep outside. He mentally scanned his notes, attempting to find the answer to his confusion.

"Is this the famed room with a sickly reputation," he muttered, wiping the film of dust off the windowpane. He stared down into the courtyard below and saw a woman. Her words, barely audible, floated up to him through the broken panes.

Help me! Save me!

"Son of a specter's uncle! That's just great, another possible victim!" Joe spun on his heels—and abruptly found himself struggling for breath, his hand flying to the holster attached to his side. He found it difficult to inhale as his gaze moved up from the dangling feet to the swollen belly, upward to the rope fit snugly around the pale throat, hanging from the piping at the top of the ceiling.

"Oh my God!"

Joe inched slowly toward the body, his eyes widening in disbelief; the drumming of his heart keeping an odd rhythmic time with the sliding, scrape-scratch of his feet against the aged planks of the floor. He lifted a hand toward the stockinged foot, then stopped and sucked in a huge breath when it vanished before his eyes. He shook his head to clear his mind and dashed back to the window.

A look down into the courtyard confirmed the suspicion spiraling in his head—the woman that had run, yelling, was gone. "No doubt gone long ago." Still, he needed to be certain that the house hadn't devoured yet another curious ghost seeker, and the only way to do that was to make a complete sweep of the house and grounds.

"Ok, so now that you've garnered my attention," Joe said, looking at the ceiling, "mind explaining what it is you've been trying to tell everybody—preferably without killing me in the process?"

Joe shrugged at the silly feeling that swept over him, at talking to a building, but the way he figured it, it couldn't hurt to be on good terms with a bully that was far bigger, meaner, and stronger. He wasn't surprised, but remained slightly disappointed, when the sanatorium didn't reply to his query. If there were ghosts inhabiting this place, they seemed to be extremely picky on who to let live and who to do away with. He felt fortunate that, for the time being, he was on the let-him-live list.

He braced his nerves and stepped back into the corridor.

"Please don't leave me here."

The whispered plea was uttered so softly that Joe thought it was an auditory illusion caused by the wind whistling through the broken pane, but had there been any wind? He glanced down at his arms and saw the hair bristling. He felt the hairs on his neck bristling also, and while the temperature had noticeably dropped, he wasn't excessively cold or exceptionally anxious. The tingling along his spine felt like a mild electric charge, as if there were an unseen energy force sweeping over his body. It caused him to jerk spasmodically, as if someone had run a finger along his backbone, tickling him.

He drew in a deep, calming breath, and turned slowly to face the room again, half expecting the hanging woman's eyes to be open and the whispered plea to be repeated from her bluish, swollen lips. He didn't know how he'd react in that instance, but he was certain he'd likely react poorly.

He was more than a little surprised when he saw a stunning young woman in a white gown seated on the bed. Her gaze met his with a directness that startled him, the orbs filled with fear and desperation. Her dark hair lay disheveled about her pale, nearly translucent face. He glanced down, his gaze drawn to the blood staining the gown around her wrists and down the front panel. Apparent suicide, he thought immediately. Had he not known she was a ghostly apparition, he would think her as real as himself, and dash her off to a hospital for treatment. He moved slowly toward a nearby chair, worried that any sudden movement might startle her like a deer, and she'd bolt back to the invisible woods of Ghostville, or wherever the dearly departed gallivanted about when unseen by the living.

He realized soon enough that his concern was unfounded, as she continued to stare at him, a pleading in her gaze that ripped through his heart. He settled slowly on the seat and waited, his gaze refusing to leave her own. He would sit as long as need be until she felt safe enough to speak with him but was relieved that he didn't have to wait long.

"FBI?"

"Sheriff."

"Please don't leave me here," she whispered again, and Joe saw a lone tear escape from her azure eyes.

"I won't." Joe's gaze moved over her face and a sense of recognition swept over him. She looked like someone he knew. "Can you help me understand what happened here? To you?"

She looked down, her brow knitted in fear and confusion, and her translucent skin took on an air of transparency. He quickly backtracked and changed his tact, hoping to keep her corporeal for just a while longer. "Why don't we just start with what you may know, or might be able to tell me? Can you tell me your name?" Joe kept his tone as reassuring as if trying to coax a kitten from a tree.

"Maria."

Joe sighed audibly, pleased that she returned to her physical state, "I want you to know that I'm here to help you, Maria, but if there is something that you can't remember or don't wish to talk about, just let me know. No vanishing, okay?" He smiled softly and was pleased to see her nod slightly. He sighed again, only just realizing that interviewing a ghost was even trickier than interviewing a witness, a victim, or a perp. At least with the latter three, he could keep them in the room until the interview concluded. With Maria, she could vanish at the blink of an eye. He needed to tread softly. He just wished he didn't feel as if he were treading on quicksand.

"Do you happen to remember your last name, Maria, and don't forget, you don't need to answer if you don't choose to, okay?"

"Bartonelli." Her reply was as immediate as was his reaction. Joe forced his features to remain neutral, but his mind and heart were racing on a collision course with the reality of what he'd just heard. Seated before him was the relative of Mandy Bartonelli, of that he was certain; and with that certainty came the certainty as to why Mandy hired the Specter Detectors. She wanted answers, just as he did. Answers to questions about what had happened to her great—whatever the relationship was. He wondered whether Maria knew of Mandy's recent visit, or if she was privy to information surrounding the deaths of so many people. He suddenly had the overwhelming urge to bombard Maria with the proverbial thousand-and-one questions, but just as he kept his facial expressions neutral, he forced his mind into park. He couldn't risk scaring this woman, who had already suffered so greatly. He took a deep breath and forced his tone to remain calm and reassuring.

"You asked me not to leave you here, Maria. Is there a reason why you can't leave on your own?" He wanted to ask if there was not some light that she could make her way towards, but he couldn't bring himself to sound flippant. Not now when she was putting her faith in him; faith enough to stay and talk to him anyway, to trust him to help her find release—whatever that might look like.

"They won't let me," Maria whispered, and Joe could hear the terror in her voice.

Suddenly, Joe didn't much care about who "they" were, or that he sat here in a haunted nuthouse talking to a ghost. All he heard was fear in her tone and every instinct, down to the marrow of his bones, to serve and protect, kicked in, putting him in a mood to kick some phantasmal ass. As with his earlier reaction, he quickly reigned in his emotions and forced himself to remain calm.

"Try to help me work through my confusion, Maria. Can you help me do that?"

Maria cocked her head but remained silent.

"You want to leave, but are afraid because someone won't allow it, but how do you know they won't allow you to leave? Have you tried to leave before?"

Maria pulled her knees up and wrapped her arms around them in what Joe perceived to be a protective measure. She rested her chin on her arms and stared at the floor, her body rocking gently, then soon after began humming quietly. There was no recognizable tune, only a faint droning sound, which tugged at the sheriff's heartstrings even more, making him wish he could go wrap his arms in comfort around her, allow her to draw strength from him.

Just as much, he wanted to retract the question, but his need for answers kept his tongue firmly in check. He remained as silent as Maria was, patiently waiting, hoping she'd stay; hoping she'd feel compelled to answer.

THIRTY-TWO

Joe's gaze remained resolutely affixed on the beauteous phantom seated, now in silence, swaying gently. In his peripheral vision, he could see the hues in the sky change from blue to burnt orange as the sun moved slowly across the horizon. He was concerned about staying in this place after dark, but his fascination with Maria, and the fact that he was conversing with a ghost, kept his body firmly seated on the chair. *A hard chair* his mind supplied, when Joe shifted slightly and felt a numbing tingle shoot through his butt cheeks. He moaned.

The noise must have startled Maria, for she jerked and brought her gaze back to bear on Joe. She seemed unfazed over the passage of time, unlike him.

"Feel like continuing our conversation?" He asked, his voice breaking on a croak. He had sat in silence for the better part of four hours and had to swallow several times to lubricate his vocal cords again. "Thank you for staying," he said after another minute, and smiled when a tiny smile broke at the corner of her lips.

"Where else would I go?" She asked, and he grinned at her ironic tone. Was she truly aware that she was a ghost trapped between worlds, or was her mind simply reliving her time of entrapment here, when freedom was unattainable?

"How many people have tried to help you leave here before me, Maria?" Joe asked again, hoping she would not curl into a ball and become uncommunicative again.

"Four."

"You said that someone wouldn't let you leave?"

"Yes." Her response was accompanied by a worried glance toward the door, as if she anticipated that their continued conversation would draw the unwanted attention of those who held her captive.

"How did they stop those four people from helping you? You were going to tell me that something happened to the other people that tried to help you, weren't you?"

Maria shook her head.

"Okay, can you tell me about the four people then? They were nice, weren't they? They tried to help you."

Maria nodded, and tears welled in her eyes.

Joe sighed again and fell silent. He was surprised at how little this conversation had gone thus far and was grateful that the good Lord had instilled in him the patience required for being a Sheriff. Another hour passed and the shadows in the room grew denser as the sun moved lower on the horizon. He couldn't push Maria for answers but needed to stay to try to get those answers, or she may never make herself available again. He had little option if he wanted to close every open murder case in his file—all five of them. Despite the danger to himself, he had to stay.

"Did all four of those people try to help you together?" He asked, trying to pry free the answers without damaging her more than she'd already been damaged.

Maria shook her head.

"Okay, so they were all here at different times, then?"

Maria shook her head again, and Joe's brow knitted in confusion. Non-committal responses & teeth-pulling interrogations must run in the Bartonelli family because he was having as difficult a time drawing answers from Maria as he did from her relative, Mandy. Yep, he felt himself fortunate to have been instilled with the patience of the gods, but had he wanted to pull teeth, he would have gone to dental school. He and Maria sighed at the same time, and he grinned, which brought another small smile to Maria's normally reticent features.

Maria took a deep breath and finally spoke again.

"The first to try to help…" she began.

THIRTY-THREE

October 1927

"I'm telling you right now," the FBI agent reported sternly, "that I am not guessing about Maria Bartonelli's whereabouts, I know that she's here. Her father stashed her here to keep me from interviewing her about the death of her mother. Now do you bring her to me, Dr. Santanini, or do I return in an hour with a dozen federal officers?"

"You can return with whomever you please, but you'll not find Maria Bartonelli here," Dr. Santanini replied smugly, then thought tacitly, *because I'll have her removed from the premises by then.*

"If you think you're protecting the money paid to you by Arthur Bartonelli, to stash his daughter here, I'm telling you right now that we'll be confiscating all your assets as an accessory to kidnapping and murder, once we've questioned Maria Bartonelli and she rats her father out. And before you deny your involvement and any knowledge of her whereabouts again," the agent persisted smugly, "I'll advise you that Lorenzo Bartonelli, Maria's brother, has already come to us and told us all about what their father did, so there's no more shield to hide behind. Now where is she?"

"Help me, save me!" The FBI stopped his threats when he heard the cries, the distress in the words obvious. "Help me, save me!" He turned to find the source of the plea and saw a woman running from the building. Against the white of her gown was the easily discernable redness of blood staining the material at the wrists and splotching the front. He squinted as familiarity began to register and then his eyes widened, and he spun to face Dr. Santanini again.

"You son-of-a-bitch," the agent snapped at Dr. Santanini, when he noticed Maria's disheveled appearance. "I'll have you strapped to the electric chair for this," he snarled.

"I had nothing to do with—" Dr. Santanini started to protest, but the agent had turned and was moving quickly toward Maria. His pace quickened when he noticed that she was being pursued by a burly man in an orderly's uniform, and coming at her from another direction were two more orderlies, who'd obviously heard her calls just as he had. He urged her to keep moving toward him, but instead she veered away. His brow knitted in confusion over her actions, and he wondered whether the loss of blood was affecting her ability to think straight.

Maria wanted to laugh for joy but was too busy trying to stay upright; to keep her mind focused on getting to the FBI agent. She knew it was him because his face was etched permanently in her memory—as both the inadvertent cause of her mother's death and of her imprisonment. Still, he was also the only one who could see her freed from this place.

"Please, help me, please, save me!" She screamed repeatedly, hoarsely, scared that if she ceased her pleas, the agent would somehow decide to forget about her; but he had seen her and was making his way in her direction. She stumbled and fell. The pain threatened to engulf her in a dark void of insentience, but her determination to be free propelled her forward. She pushed herself onto her feet, swaying precariously. She closed her eyes and drew in a deep breath of determination and then started towards the FBI agent again. *How far away could he be?* She wondered, not realizing that several hundred feet separated the rescuer from the captive.

Something in her periphery caught her attention and she groaned. Two more orderlies were heading toward her from the side of the building. They'd intercept her long before the agent got to her. If she could only stay away from the orderlies, just long enough for the agent to catch up with her—

She veered toward the cliffs.

The agent saw the three men headed toward Maria Bartonelli and anger welled inside him. He yelled over his shoulder at Dr.

Santanini, "Call off the dogs!"

Dr. Santanini lifted his chin and did not acknowledge the command. The agent drew in a deep breath of anger, pulled his gun, and screamed at the men, "FBI. Stay where you are!" None did. It was if they were more afraid not to retrieve their captive, than of an FBI agent.

He stopped moving, took aim and fired, striking one man in the thigh. Orderly number one fell in a cry of anguish. The agent took aim and yelled again, "Halt, or I'll shoot every one of you where you stand!"

They continued to ignore him, rather chose to continue their single-minded pursuit of Maria, who was stumbling precariously towards the cliff. He took aim and fired again, striking the second chaser in the arm. The man gripped his arm and turned to see the FBI agent; gun still pointed in his direction. He threw up his good arm in surrender and knelt to prove he wouldn't move any further. The FBI's anger continued to elevate at having to stop, aim, and fire his weapon. It meant a delay in reaching Maria, who'd ceased crying out and was stumbling determinedly in the only direction in which an orderly wasn't. So focused was she that she didn't react to his gunfire, nor did she seem to register that those following were being dealt with.

The agent turned his attention back to the final man, still doggedly following Maria.

"Halt!" He screamed, wondering how dense these men were that they would prefer a bullet to living, because this man kept walking, but oddly had slowed his pace. That struck him as odd, because he no longer appeared to be attempting to apprehend Maria, rather seemed to be goading her…closer to the cliffs.

"Maria," he yelled, walking at a rapid pace, trying to keep his gun arm steady, "stop running. Stop!" Just as with the gunfire, she seemed oblivious. She just kept stumbling away. The FBI agent stopped walking again, aimed, and fired a final shot, hitting the last man in the back. He jerked as if punched, stumbled, and then tumbled over, face-first into the grass.

"Maria, stop!" He yelled again, then took off running after her, but it was too late. She'd moved too close to the cliffs, lost too much blood, was swaying too heavily. Without the slightest attempt to prevent it, she swayed a final time and plummeted over the edge.

THIRTY-FOUR

October 2000

Joe sat back and tried to absorb all she'd relayed, "So, the FBI tried to help you, but there were men…"

"Jekyll and Hyde," she interjected. "They were the men that Dr. Santanini put in charge of guarding me."

And no doubt other fictional bogeymen too, he thought, wiping a hand across his brow. He didn't know what he expected, but for her to relay such a heart-breaking accounting of her existence; to die so wretchedly, and then to state that her captors, the ones who caused her so much misery, were fictional characters created by Robert Louis Stephenson in eighteen-eighty-six. So much for much-needed answers. He'd just wasted five hours of his time only to discover that this woman truly had been interned here for reasons of mental defect. *Christ! Jekyll and Hyde? She probably ate dinner with Little Bo Peep and went for walks with Tom Thumb.* Still, if events of that nature actually had occurred, that would mean she had just recounted the night she died.

While he was fascinated at having conversed with an actual dead person, he needed to conclude this part of his investigation and begin anew the morrow. He stood and was startled at the rush of blood flowing through his limbs, both of which had fallen asleep.

"Please don't leave me here. The FBI man left me here."

Joe closed his eyes and tried to focus past the pain in her voice. He wasn't the FBI, and he certainly had no way to help with any closure she may be seeking; closure that the FBI would have likely given her. And he certainly had no way of "freeing" her as the FBI would have likely done. She was dead, and her death happened so many decades prior that there was no one to bring to justice any longer. Right now, he had to focus on the recently deceased.

Joe finally opened his eyes and tested to see if his legs would carry him now that the painful tingly numbness had passed. He took a tentative step and was pleased his legs didn't buckle beneath him. He looked back at Maria who had moved to stand before him. *Just a waif of a girl,* he thought. *The top of her head barely reaches my chin. Who could harm her? Why would they harm her?*

"I promised that I wouldn't leave you here, and I won't," he answered, sighing inwardly; but wondered just how he was truly supposed to help her leave. What did that entail precisely? Would he end up on the coroner's slab too if she attempted to follow him from the room? *Serve and protect* never weighed heavier on his shoulders than at this moment when a ghost was pleading for his help and an untold number of other ghosts may very well try to roast him alive. She'd said that four people had tried to help her, and it was apparent that one of those, at least in her mind, had done so when she was alive; which meant that three others had borne witness to her distress and had potentially died trying to save her, as she was now pleading with him to do; potentially one—or three of them—in his unsolved case file.

Was she even aware of what she was asking him to do? What she'd asked of the others? Was she aware that asking could cost him his life?

"Do you have any suggestions, Maria?"

Maria's eyebrows knitted and her lips puckered. As before, silence accompanied her confused daze.

"You said that Jekyll and Hyde," he started, shaking his head mentally in disbelief that he was catering that that delusion, but someone had prevented her leaving; someone had been responsible for her demise. He sighed heavily and then continued, "You said they prevented your leaving here before, and I think I'm beginning to comprehend how they prevented the last three people from helping you and have probably harmed many others over the decades: people I'm not even aware of. Recently, three people came here," he continued, "and entities lit your room on fire somehow and burned those three innocents to death. That isn't exactly a fate I have in store for myself."

"My room? No. I have seen only one man recently, and he did not die by fire," Maria said, the perplexity upon her face genuine.

"Do you know his name, and how he died?" Joe asked, settling reluctantly back onto the chair, now knowing that by his revealing the information he had, he had re-opened questions into inquiries he'd assumed he'd just solved. Maria looked down at him and moved to sit on her bed again.

"I think he said his name was Kevin," she whispered, "but he was not here long before Jekyll and Hyde decided he was intruding. They grabbed him, flung him mercilessly about the room—over and over; then drug him from here to the fourth floor…"

"The autopsy room?"

Maria shook her head, "No, the autopsy room is not on the fourth floor, the fourth floor is where they all end up though; where Jekyll and Hyde drag them to the doctors so they can conduct their foul experiments before the poor souls end up dying and being fed to the ocean."

"Can you tell me who the other two were? The other two that tried to help you?"

"I only know that Jekyll and Hyde stopped them just as brutally as they did Kevin. Poor Kevin. He kept asking me questions, but I was so afraid to answer them for fear that if I did, Jekyll or Hyde would hear."

"Then how do you know he was here to help you escape?" Joe asked, confused.

"Why else would you have come to my room?" Maria asked, a perplexing look on her features. "I only wished he'd have not stayed so long. Then Jekyll or Hyde would maybe have left him alone.

Others that walked near, but did not dwell, left alive—" Maria fell silent, renewed sadness on her countenance.

The fact that she kept referring to these two people by those of fictional characters had him concerned that her recall was skewed by mental deficiency; yet she sounded so lucid and sane, and there were times he forgot that he was actually conversing with a ghost. There was only one way he knew to find out whether she was loopy, and that was direct inquiry, "You keep calling these people—ghosts now, I guess—Jekyll and Hyde…"

"They were the guards assigned to me," Maria interrupted. "Anytime anyone from the outside came searching for me, they were to stop them talking to me. Even if the law didn't come looking for me, I was guarded to keep from making my presence known. Confined me to my room and stood guard until the law left the building. Anytime I tried to escape, they were there to prevent it. The last time I got away but ended trapped here just the same. I only refer to them as such, because I don't know their real names, and they remind me of the characters I read about in the book by Robert Lewis Stevenson."

Joe breathed a sigh of relief that her references made sense; but then his brow knitted in confusion at Maria's cryptic words. *The last time I got away*, she'd said. His eyes widened as her meaning registered—during her final escape attempt, she'd "gotten away" by running over a cliff; however, her ghost ended ensnared in the same hellhole she'd suffered in life. Apparently, when her guards died, they too remained confined at the institution, thereby tormenting Maria in death as they had in life. He groaned at the injustice dealt this poor girl—in life and in death.

"Why were you sent here, Maria? You said the FBI wanted to find you to question you because of something that happened, but you didn't say what."

"Because my father killed my mother, and I saw it happen," she whispered, the pain in her tone sharp. "My father knew I would never lie if asked, so to keep the FBI from asking, he sent me here; then paid Dr. Santanini a lot of money to have Jekyll and Hyde guard me night and day—"

"Oh my God!"

She continued speaking, her voice dropping to a whisper, "but it isn't just Jekyll and Hyde determined to keep me and others here; there are other guards, and the doctors who continue to perform tests and experiments on the poor souls trapped here too. Every day, we hear repeated screams of those who suffer in a never-ending torment. Occasionally, we hear new screams from those living who dare enter this place. Those who dare attempt to help those trapped here; dare to try to help the ones who wouldn't harm a soul; the ones just trying to find release from our imprisonment."

"Like you, Maria?"

"Like me."

"There's one other thing that's really bugging me, Maria, and maybe you can help to clear it up a bit."

Maria looked at him questioningly but didn't respond.

"Back in nineteen-sixty-four, a doctor by the name of Jeff Markus, converted this place into a geriatric facility. Why were so many people permitted to live here, to visit here during the nine years the place was opened? Were there just too many people for the ghosts to get rid of? Do you know anything about that time that I'm referring to?"

Maria had begun nodding when he'd asked his first question and was more than happy to talk about the old folks that lived there, "During that time, things were happy here. Many of us were able to move about and talk with the old people. I met my relative here, someone I hadn't seen since…well…before I was snatched away from my home. Her name was Rebecca, and she was married to my

169

brother, Lorenzo. It was so good to see Becca again, but it took me a long time to decide to talk to her, because I was so afraid—"

"That Jekyll or Hyde would kill her."

Maria nodded, "But there were priests here often, blessing the facility." Joe's brow knitted at that, so Maria tried to explain, "You mentioned a Dr. Markus."

Joe nodded, and Maria continued. "He knew we were here and since he didn't know what to do about us, he called in priests to come bless the facility every week. He thought that, if he did that, it would prevent any harm from befalling the residence here; thought that it might make us leave."

"I guess the leaving part didn't happen, but did it prevent the elderly from being injured?"

"I don't know if that was why, or if it was as you said—that there were simply too many people around all the time. All I know is that for those years that Becca was here, I had a friend again. We would often sit in my…our…room, and talk, just as we did before Dad killed Mom. Then all the elderly living here started getting sick—really sick—and then they were gone, and everything went back to before—"

"Then we need to find a way to get you out of here so you can move on to a happier place. All we need to do is give those poltergeists the slip," Joe smiled encouragingly, but his heart began to bang away again, like a runaway freight train.

"I truly do not understand how you've managed to stay inside this building as long as you have," Maria stated her surprise over their extended conversation. "Are you sure you're alive?"

Joe laughed. It felt good to laugh. He hadn't laughed sincerely since those young men vanished in nineteen ninety-three—at least not that he could recall. A grin here and there, but not genuine laughter. Still, he had to wonder why he was still alive *to* laugh, and why he was able to talk to Maria, when cantankerous ghouls had brutally executed others before him.

"I don't know, Maria, but I am certainly not going to create a scene and insist some foul-tempered phantom fricassee me. I think it's best we do not draw attention to ourselves. I'll just casually make my way toward the front door, and you follow behind nonchalantly. See if we can't pull the wool over the eyes of the guards. Still, I don't know what we'll do once we get you there. Do you follow the light, or—"

Maria giggled, then grew somber again, "I truly do not know, because I've never been set free. If we make it outside and no one kills you, maybe true freedom will come, but I worry that you'll die— like the others—and I'll once again be—"

"Let's try to dwell on the positive, okay? I'm alive right now, and have been for several hours now, so there has to be a reason why they're not attacking me."

Maria's gaze drifted to the badge on his shirt, "Perhaps they're leaving you alone because you're a lawman," Maria exclaimed. "They always lie low when the law comes. Maybe even now they fear you because of the fear they've always known."

"Well, let's hope you're right, because I don't want to become some sick phantom's next barbecued victim. I'm going to step out into the corridor to see if it's clear. You stay here and watch for my signal to follow along—and Maria?"

"Yes."

"Pray that the floor doesn't ignite."

THIRTY-FIVE

Sheriff Joe Montgomery stepped to the door of the room and peered out, his heart resuming the thudding race of fear that it had when he first encountered the pregnant woman hanging in the room behind him. Standing smack dab in the middle of the corridor were dozens of men—some dressed in gray orderly uniforms, some in white's doctor's frocks; all wearing frowns of displeasure. As a sheriff, he shouldn't be afraid, but as a sheriff, he'd never found himself facing down a horde of poltergeists with a determination to potentially do him harm.

"We were hoping that you would not remain," an orderly near the front of the group said, his tone a menace that promised retribution for his intrusion. "The patients that reside here are not your concern, lawman."

Maria had been right, the ghosts seemed disinclined to bother a man of the law, but for how long would that respect or fear last?

For the first time in his career, the sheriff was dumbfounded and uncertain how to proceed. These were not criminals, whom he could simply slap the handcuffs on and haul off to prison. These were ghosts, trapped in time, and still performing a sworn duty to their prior employer; and they could snuff out his life with the flick of an invisible switch; at least that's how Maria Bartonelli and Parker Wentworth had described it.

He instinctively glanced at the floor, relieved that it hadn't begun glowing red hot. In his mind, he tried to formulate a plan. Should he act brave and unaffected; demand that they release their hold on Maria and the others? Or, try tact and plead for their release; and his as well? The police academy certainly never prepared him for this; neither had his life experiences. He took a deep breath, and then released it slowly, his gaze scanning the faces of the orderlies and doctors standing before him.

Apparently, they wished to continue conducting their experiments and living here, as they'd done in life; they knew nothing different. Did he really have grounds to prevent that? How did one go about explaining to a ghost that their behavior was reprehensible and potentially illegal? Was it illegal? Did the law apply to the dead harming the dead? It wasn't as if they had a reason to fear the law—anymore. Then again, the killing of those *not* long dead was definitely illegal, which brought him back around to what he could actually do about it.

The ghosts continued to stand and stare at him, blocking the hallway to prevent his departure. Could he simply walk through them? Would they even permit that? As with most of what had occurred today, he had nothing in his experience to draw from. Showdowns he'd had before, but never any like this.

As with Maria, the passage of time appeared inconsequential; as did blinking, apparently. It was unnerving at the very least to stand face-to-face with non-blinking entities with a penchant for carnage.

As he stared into their vacant expressions, the proverbial light bulb lit in his mind, and the sheriff decided upon a course of action.

"I came to take Maria down to the station for questioning. Apparently, she was witness to a homicide. She needs to come with me. Maria?" Joe reached behind himself instinctively but would not have been able to ascertain whether she was placing her ghostly hand into his or not, but at the same time, to turn his gaze from the threat before him to check would be reckless; careless. For all he knew, Maria could have vanished the moment these hoodlums in hospital attire appeared. He hoped not. He would hate to think that he'd made her a promise of freedom only to be unable to deliver on that promise. Did she trust in him, and his badge, enough to stand firm and walk from this place by his side? He hoped so.

He also hoped that the obvious respect, or fear, of the law during the time that these men were alive had carried over into the present day and they would not attempt to prevent him performing his own duty. They hadn't thus far. He felt absurd in his pretense, but his badge—and feigned assurance—was all he had to work with.

"No one leaves without Doctor Santanini's express consent," the orderly snapped, taking a step closer.

"You must not have been on duty when I first arrived, and obviously weren't here before Dr. Santanini departed for the day, or you would have known that he already *gave* his consent," Joe lied smoothly. "I would have transported her to the station already but decided to obtain a preliminary statement here beforehand. Now, if you all would just step aside, we need to be on our way. Or do I need to arrest you all for obstruction of justice?"

Good Lord, but he felt preposterous, speaking to dead people as though they were a mere mob, an inconvenience. Did it register to these ghosts that his threats were hollow? That he couldn't do anything to them because they were already dead? Surely, if they were concerned over anything they might have done in life—and after death—they'd not be standing here eyeing him with the caution that the living reserve for the law—when it's respected or feared.

Their behavior was a conundrum that he'd sort out later, once he was safely away from this place. For now, he'd continue hoping that his badge held sway over them, and they kept their distance.

He took a step forward, hoping that his pace didn't appear tentative and that he exuded his normal confidence of authority.

His assurance intensified as the mob slowly parted, albeit with a unified disgruntled demeanor. Once more he fought the urge to check behind him to see if Maria was following, holding his hand. For all he knew, the ghosts were aware that he had no one accompanying him and would have a good chortle at his expense once he exited this floor. In that event, he hadn't a doubt that the chances of his returning to retrieve Maria a second time would not prove successful. If he didn't have Maria in tow, that may also be why they were allowing him to walk out of here with his hide still pink and fleshy.

"How did you know I witnessed my mother's murder?" A voice whispered against the back of his head, and it took sheer willpower not to react by jumping out of his skin.

He let go his breath with an audible whoosh, a triumphant grin spreading across his face. She was with him, and they were nearing the elevator without any interference. "Don't you remember telling me, Maria?" He whispered. He still dared not look behind him but could somehow sense her shake her head.

"I will answer your questions when we get outside, ok? Right now, just stay close to me." He didn't know whether people developed super-hearing capabilities after they passed or not, but he wasn't about to risk the guards overhearing a conversation which may make them doubt the veracity of his claim for taking a resident out of their custody and into his.

He depressed the down arrow on the elevator, the scratch of disuse music to his ears. The louder the rusted scraping, the nearer the elevator, the greater the chances of their leaving alive. In reality he hated the thought of climbing aboard the antiquated elevator; fear that had him taking the stairs earlier, upon his arrival. But now, climbing into that box, knowing that those doors would slip close, and it would transport him to the bottom floor more rapidly than traversing five flights of stairs.

The elevator stopped and the doors slowly parted. With a final glance over his shoulders at the employees of Monterey Cliffs Sanatorium, he stepped into the box, but didn't release the breath he'd been holding until the doors slid closed behind them.

"Thank you," Maria whispered.

Only then did Joe look down to see that Maria had indeed placed her hand in his, and her confidence as well. He smiled—not only because he had succeeded in freeing this wretched soul from an eternity in Hell, but because he could finally close at least one of the files on the disappearances that had occurred here back in ninety-three and could say with just about as much certainty that Amanda and Parker were not certifiably insane—nor was Joey Trist.

"Just doing my job, little lady. Just doing my job."

Joe felt sweat pop out along his upper lip at the same time the elevator released a groaning wail. He swiped at the sweat lining his brow, furrowed with concern at the sudden rise in temperature. Then came the deafening sound of the cable snapping, and their freefall began.

THIRTY-SIX

He should have been able to walk away. The drop had only been four floors, but the doors refused to budge. He was trapped, and the heat was intensifying. For reasons he couldn't begin to fathom, Maria sat by his side, a look of abject fear in her eyes, as if her fate was to die again and return as a prisoner to room *502* for all eternity. Didn't she know that her corporeal state was an illusion? That she could escape her imprisonment by simply walking through the elevator doors?

"Maria! There's no need for you to stay by my side. We are on the ground floor. The front doors are only a few steps away. There's no one to stop you now. You're free. Get out! Go!" He didn't know whether that was true or not; would simply running out the front doors release her from the grip of the sanatorium? Had she not run before, in her ghostly form, many times prior, only to return to room *502* just as swiftly? Perhaps his giving her permission was all she needed to break the loop; the cycle of flee and return. Perhaps if she walked out, she could truly keep on going. It was only a hope, but he needed that hope at this moment; because something told him she would need to believe in her freedom; the freedom he'd worked so hard to attain for her.

Maria turned to look at Joe, tears streaming down her cheeks, "You died to save me."

"Oh, little girl, I'm not dead yet!" There was that damnable confidence of his that he used to deliver comfort, when inside he knew his fate was sealed as tightly as were the elevator doors. Sweat was pouring from every pore as the walls and the floor grew warmer. Why were the demons within this facility toying with him? Why not just do to him what they'd done to others—roast him like a pig on a spit! Why increase the heat by degrees? Did they want him to suffer? Make him pay for taking away one of their own? If so, why did they wait until he was in the elevator? Why not take him out when he was on the fifth floor?

"Because I had a chance of escaping from the fifth floor," he muttered, "whereas my chances of escaping from this elevator are slim to none. Something about killing a lawman face-to-face wasn't something even poltergeists were capable of doing, so just like any cowards, they waited until my back was turned. Sons-of-bitches!"

Maria nodded solemnly and slowly began to fade.

"Promise me you'll make a break for it, Maria. Leave this place. Don't let them win!"

"I promise," Maria's form becoming more translucent. "I am ready to go. I just wish that you could come with me."

"Maybe I will see you on the outside, before you disappear into whatever light or portal shows up that's meant to carry you to your final resting place, eh?" Joe wanted to smile encouragingly, but his brow furrowed in distress over the raspy sound of his voice. The heat was beginning to affect his vocal cords. "Go on, now!" He squeezed his eyes tight to try to produce tears to ease the burning in his eyes, but the ducts had dried up. When he opened them, he was alone—and scared.

THIRTY-SEVEN

"I can't believe we're coming back up here! Are you sure you haven't lost your marbles, Mandy?" Parker was gripping the door tightly, as Mandy whipped around the bends leading up to the sanatorium, the lights of a deputy's vehicle in close pursuit, illuminating the interior of her Jaguar an eerie red and blue.

"Sheriff Montgomery has been gone all day, without checking in. I'll be damned if I'm going to sit by and allow the ghosts in that building to claim yet another life. Not without doing everything I can to stop it!"

"Do you hear yourself, Mandy? Exactly what is it you think we can do? I hate to break it to you, sweetheart, but if it comes down to a battle, you and I—and Barney Fife in that cop car back there—don't stand a chance in Hades!"

"I don't know, Parker. I hear what you're saying, but after seeing what happened to the Specter Detectors; knowing that those same fiends caused the death of Stephen and his friends and knowing that Sheriff Montgomery could be lying in that place dead or dying...I can't just sit back and do nothing."

"I know, but I'm at a loss as to what that something would be."

"We'll just have to take it as it comes."

"I just wish I had packed my ghost-busting gear before we left," Parker grinned nervously as they rounded the final bend in the road. The beam from the headlights fell upon a figure in white staring up at the sanatorium.

"Oh my God!" Mandy and Parker said simultaneously.

Mandy threw the car into park, but without bothering to shut off the ignition, she leapt from the vehicle, with Parker following close behind. She was making a beeline towards the front door, when the figure in white suddenly appeared before her, blocking her way.

"You cannot go inside."

Mandy was stunned, both that an apparition was talking to her, and that the apparition could very well be her twin sister. After all these years, she was certain that she was standing face-to-face with her grand-aunt Maria. Her Grannie Becca had been right after all. Maria had been interned in this facility in the twenties, which meant that her family lied about how and why she died. She hoped that Maria would stay around long enough to answer some questions, but right now, she needed to get inside to try to find Sheriff Montgomery.

"Holy crap!" Parker said, skidding to a halt beside Mandy. "Isn't she the grand aunt you were telling me about, Mandy? She looks more like you in person than she did in that picture you showed me!"

Maria and Mandy looked at Parker, but neither spoke until Mandy attempted to sidestep Maria and head for the building again.

"You cannot go inside," Maria asserted, moving to block Mandy again.

"Maria, you have to let me in. If there's the slightest chance of saving the sheriff," Mandy implored. "He *is* in there, isn't he?"

"I'd like to know the answer to that also," the deputy said, moving to stand next to Parker. "Can you enlighten us, miss?"

"You know you're talking to a ghost, right?" Parker whispered to the deputy.

The deputy blinked rapidly, his jaw dropping as the realization hit him, "Holy Frijoles!"

"Precisely my reaction," Parker replied.

"Please Maria, let us help him. You know the sheriff, don't you?" Mandy asked, her fear elevating with each passing moment that they stood outside. She had to get past Maria, but she didn't know if she'd be able to.

"The sheriff. Yes, I know him. He saved my life. He helped me when no one else could," Maria whispered, tears welling in her eyes again. "He will not be coming out of the building alive. I am waiting for him, so we may go away from here together. If you go inside, I fear the others will not let you live either. They are very angry with the sheriff for taking me away. They have him trapped in the elevator…"

Mandy didn't wait to hear anything further. She took the risk and dashed around Maria before her grandaunt could move into her path again, bolting for the front door.

"Mandy!" Parker yelled, chasing after her.

Maria stood beside the deputy, who continued to gawk at her disbelieving, "They will not live," she whispered sadly, jolting the deputy out of his stupor. He looked toward the building and ran in the direction the other two had gone. He didn't know what he would be up against, but he couldn't let two civilians face an unknown danger alone; especially when it was his boss they were trying to save.

When he entered the building, he immediately spotted Mandy and Parker over by the elevator. He ran over to help, but they stopped him.

"Don't touch it! It's fire hot," Parker snapped. "Try to find something sturdy we can wedge in between the doors."

The deputy quickly spun, looking for anything thin and strong that he could utilize. Parker and Mandy started searching also, knowing that with each minute that ticked by the sheriff's life was at greater risk. Parker tossed aside chairs, hurling them angrily in his frustration.

"Found something," Mandy called, racing from one of the first-floor offices, holding a thin pipe, the end of which was miraculously flattened, as if a higher power wanted them to save the sheriff. "Must have fallen from the ceiling," she said, running toward the elevator. "Please fit," she murmured, pushing the collapsed end in between the doors.

Parker and the deputy raced over and applied the needed torque until the narrow piping slid in between the doors. All three grunted mightily, pushing and tugging until the doors unwillingly parted, revealing the burnt corpse of the sheriff, lying in a heap against the wall of the elevator car.

"I am sorry for his death. He was a good man," Maria whispered, peering into the car, "but you must leave now. I hear them coming. They will not be kind."

Just then the sheriff let loose a small, nearly imperceptible groan, which snapped everyone out of their disbelief.

"Grab his legs, and I'll grab him under the arms," the deputy commanded Parker, who immediately stepped inside to do as instructed.

Maria paced the area, wringing her hands, "Please," she pleaded. "You must leave."

"We're trying," the deputy snapped. After several attempts, the two men hefted the sheriff's much larger frame and headed toward the outside. Mandy raced along ahead to open the door. She pushed it open and then turned to wait for Parker and the deputy. The sight that met her when she turned caused her heart to skip a beat and a lump to form in her throat. At the top of the stairwell were dozens of figures, and they were glaring at them.

"Hurry!" She cried, as the throng of apparitions started menacingly towards them.

Maria moved closer to the staircase, a lone force standing between two determined rivals. She screamed at them, which startled them into stopping, "Is it not enough that you've already killed one lawman? Are you really ready to kill another one? These people are only here to remove the body of that lawman; his deputy is one of them. Let them leave in peace!"

The mass parted, and the ghosts of Dr. Santanini, followed closely by Jekyll and Hyde, walked forward.

"You are the cause of all these deaths, Maria," Dr. Santanini accused. "Now return to your room and stay there." He nodded to the two orderlies who stepped forward and snared Maria by the arms, hauling her back with them toward the staircase. She'd been free, but now she was again their captive. She did not kick or scream but went with them meekly. If it meant saving these four lives, she willingly gave up hers—again.

THIRTY-EIGHT

"Get him to the car," Mandy screamed when the two men lay the sheriff down just outside the front door. "We can't stay here!"

Parker stepped over and wrapped his arms around her, "He's gone, Mandy. We felt him go limp just as we exited the building; and the other ghosts appeared to be satisfied in retrieving their prisoner, so it looks as if they've gone back to…wherever it is they hide away."

Mandy stood in her fiancé's embrace, shaking her head against his shoulder, tears falling, soaking his shirt. The sheriff had given his life trying to solve the mysterious homicides related to this place, and Maria had given her freedom so that they could live. Somehow, none of what happened seemed merited and that left her feeling hollow inside.

After a few minutes, she pulled away and wiped her tears angrily, sniffing loudly, "There isn't much else we can do," she murmured dully. "We still need to take the sheriff home. He deserves to be buried so he can be at peace."

"How are we going to explain all of this away?" The deputy muttered, wondering just how he was going to write up this particular report.

"My suggestion is to let the M.E. handle this like he's doing for the Inspector Detectors," Mandy replied. "There won't be a resolution any more than with any other incident because there's no way to explain what happened here. Never has been. And as of Monday, there will be nothing left of this place that can hurt anyone ever again. So, please…collect his body and let's go."

The men complied somberly, and soon they were headed down the road leading back to town, each trying to squeeze all memories of the night permanently from their minds; knowing they would carry the scars with them forever.

***June** 2005*

"I'm surprised you've decided to return for the grand opening," Parker reiterated a second time as he and his wife started up the road leading to the former site of the Monterey Cliffs Sanatorium.

"I can't hide from this place forever," Mandy murmured. "Neither of us could."

"Well, it's a good thing we hired a reputable contractor, because this hands-off approach to building those condominiums could have proven disastrous otherwise. A less scrupulous individual could've cut all sorts of corners, taking advantage of absentee owners like us," Parker quipped.

Mandy grinned, "You do remember that we've kept in daily contact via Skype and had our contractor giving us a virtual tour of the site, daily. I'd say we were as present as could be possible, without stepping foot on the property."

"Speaking of that, are we certain we're ready to step foot up there again?"

"Are you?" Mandy queried, eyeing her husband carefully. He kept his eyes on the road, and his features bland, but his hands gripped the wheel tightly, giving away his tension as they rounded the final bend.

"We'll find out the answer to that question in all of about two minutes," he said softly.

The car came to a stop on the newly paved parking lot; but Parker and Mandy made no effort to step from the car. They were too stunned by the transformation of the area. If they'd never been here before, they would never know that it used to house one of the most notoriously haunted facilities on the planet.

In the center of the parking lot was a beautifully manicured flower garden, and the remaining lawn had been mowed and any dirt patches filled in, making it look lush in the mid-day light. Along the cliffs was a new eight-foot brick wall with triple-paned Plexiglas viewing panes placed along at even intervals, so that people who wished to, could safely view the ocean below. There were also poplar trees and hedges lining the wall, providing further barrier from the winds that could easily wreak havoc during the winter months. But as beautiful as the landscaping was, it was the condos that truly impressed them.

Four plots of twenty four-story units each sat in elegant splendor where once sat ruins. It was a wealthy person's paradise, a full-time residence, a family's ideal, or a part-time getaway. Full service, state-of-the-art entertainment facilities were situated along each side the buildings, housing everything from Olympic-sized swimming pools, to fully equipped playgrounds; game rooms to a full-sized meeting hall with a dozen conference rooms for those who wished to bring their business home. They would cater to any who had the money to pay; for these condos did not come cheap.

"It's breathtaking," Mandy murmured.

"Yes, but better still," Parker replied, "it's completely unrecognizable. I'd say that makes it well worth the thirty-million-dollar price tag. Are you ready?"

"As I'll ever be," Mandy smiled, leaning over to place a kiss on her husband's lips. "Let's go view the Monterrey Cliffs Luxury Condo Development."

They stepped from the car and stopped again, each sucking in a deep breath before proceeding. It had been four-and-a-half years since they'd been here; and though it no longer resembled that which struck fear into their hearts, the fear still lingered there.

They caught sight of the contractor, and waved, then headed over. Today, there would be a ribbon-cutting ceremony; tomorrow, those who'd already placed a deposit on a unit, would begin to move in. Within minutes, Mandy and Parker were surrounded by a quarter-dozen journalists; all paid to run an exclusive on the new facility. They plastered on the requisite smiles and walked over.

They barely stopped moving, when the first reporter thrust a microphone in Mandy's face, "What will you tell potential owners if the history of this place is uncovered—a"

"Which it will be, because I am certain you'll be adding that to your exposé, correct?" Mandy asked lightly, even though in her mind she envisioned throttling the reporter. There was a smattering of polite laughter, but it didn't take a genius to know that the history of this particular location struck a nerve.

The reporter grinned, "It is an enormous part—"

"But you said it," Parker interjected, "it's history. While the local townsfolk enjoy batting about stories of ghosts, I can assure you that there wasn't a single report of any ghostly inhabitants the entire time these luxury condos were being erected—"

A reporter interrupted, "Which could simply mean that no one ever mentioned it. After all, no one wants to claim seeing ghosts. Might make people question their sanity—"

"Or" Mandy interjected, "the ghosts simply moved on when construction began—"

"So, you *are* claiming that the place was haunted?"

Mandy was about to respond when the temperature took a nosedive. The reporters went into a frenzy as ghosts began swarming toward them en masse. Fear was set aside in favor of "getting the footage" for the "story of the century", but it was a story that would never leave the Monterey Cliffs. Mandy and Parker screamed warnings, but were ignored, so they made a mad dash for their vehicle.

No one noticed the dark-haired woman standing alongside the far unit, blood-staining each sleeve of her dressing gown; a frown creasing her brow, "Why did you have to return?" She whispered, despondent, then turned and walked away.